That's right,
I am a book
kisser.

that's kind of
perverted or
maybe it's just
romantic and
highly
INTELLIGENT.

PRAISE FOR
THE ABSOLUTELY TRUE DIARY
OF A PART-TIME INDIAN

A National Book Award Winner

BOSTON GLOBE – HORN BOOK Award Winner

A **NEW YORK TIMES** Bestseller

An **LA TIMES** Book Award nomination

A **NEW YORK TIMES BOOK REVIEW** Notable Book (children's books)

A BookSense #1 Pick

A BookSense Bestseller

A **PUBLISHERS WEEKLY** Bestseller

An ALA Best Book for Young Adults

An NYPL Book for the Teen Age

A **BCCB** Blue Ribbon Winner

A **SCHOOL LIBRARY JOURNAL** Best Book of the Year

A **HORN BOOK** Fanfare Best Book of the Year

An Amazon.com Best Book of the Year

A **PUBLISHERS WEEKLY** Best Book of the Year

A **KIRKUS REVIEWS** Best YA Book

A NAPPA Gold Award

A PNBA Book Award Winner

A Notable Book for a Global Society

A **KLIATT** Editor's Choice, Hardcover YA Fiction

An ABC Best Book for Children

A **PW** "Off the Cuff" Favorite YA Novel Award

"[**TRUE DIARY**] is Alexie's first foray into the young adult genre, and it took him only one book to master the form.... This is a gem of a book.... For fifteen years, Sherman Alexie has explored the struggle to survive between the grinding plates of the Indian and white worlds. He's done it through various characters and genres, but [**TRUE DIARY**] may be his best work yet." —**NEW YORK TIMES**

"The National Book Award–nominated **DIARY** is a remarkable tale that is sure to resonate and lift spirits of all ages for years to come." —**USA TODAY**

"When my horoscope said I was going to meet someone tall, dark and handsome...who knew he'd be fourteen! Thankfully for me, Arnold Spirit is one of the funniest, most endearing characters I've met in a very long time. This book is so original, I laughed consistently from beginning to end."

—**Amy Sedaris**, actress, comedian, and author

"Few writers are more masterful than Sherman Alexie....The high school misfit is a familiar young-adult-story template, but Alexie makes it fresh because this particular misfit is one who doesn't often appear in print." —**LOS ANGELES TIMES**

"Excellent in every way, poignant and really funny and heartwarming and honest and wise and smart....I have no doubt that in a year or so it'll both be winning awards and being banned." —Bestselling author **Neil Gaiman**

★"A Native American equivalent of ANGELA'S ASHES, a coming-of-age story so well observed that its very rootedness in one specific culture is also what lends it universality, and so emotionally honest that the humor almost always proves painful....Jazzy syntax and [Ellen] Forney's witty cartoons...transmute despair into dark humor; Alexie's no-holds-barred jokes have the effect of throwing the seriousness of his themes into high relief." —**PUBLISHERS WEEKLY** (starred review)

★"The many characters, on and off the rez, with whom [Junior] has dealings are portrayed with compassion and verve, particularly the adults in his extended family. Forney's simple pencil cartoons fit perfectly within the story and reflect the burgeoning artist within Junior." —**SCHOOL LIBRARY JOURNAL** (starred review)

"Emotionally spring-loaded, linguistically gymnastic, and devastatingly funny in turns...Alexie nails the ups and downs of a young artist learning to navigate by his own radar. Ellen Forney's inspired illustrations channel Junior's manic, tell-it-like-it-is sensibility." —**SAN FRANCISCO BAY GUARDIAN**

★"Alexie nimbly blends sharp wit with unapologetic emotion....Junior's keen cartoons sprinkle the pages as his fluid narration deftly mingles raw feeling with funny, sardonic insight." —**KIRKUS** (starred review)

★"Breathtakingly honest, funny, profane, sad...Alexie has a unique story to tell, and he tells it with raw emotion leavened with humor." —**KLIATT** (starred review)

"Fierce observations and sharp sense of humor ... The tough ideas Junior comes to terms with ... coupled with the hilarious language Alexie puts in Junior's mouth, make this an entertaining and intellectually engaging read for teens. Ellen Forney's illustrations give life to Junior's aspirations to be a cartoonist. Her drawings are so filled with Junior's personality that it is easy to think they spring from his own vivid, albeit fictional, imagination."　　—NEWSDAY

"**THE ABSOLUTELY TRUE DIARY OF A PART-TIME INDIAN** is [Alexie's] first book for young readers and it is exceptionally good.... Arnold's story is indelibly sad ... but Alexie leavens the pathos with humor, and Arnold is a wonderful character."
　　　　　　　　　　　　　　　　　　—MIAMI HERALD

"Arnold Spirit's offbeat coming-of-age tale will touch your battle-scarred teenaged heart."
　—**Megan Kelso**, cartoonist and author of **THE SQUIRREL MOTHER**

"Alexie's first novel for young adults is funny, self-deprecating, and serious all at once. With his perceptive narrator, Alexie deftly taps into the human desire to stand out while fitting in."　　—**BOOKPAGE**

"Heartbreaking, funny, and beautifully written."
　　　　　　　　—Association of Booksellers for Children

"The zest and contemporary sparkle of [**TRUE DIARY**], with art by Ellen Forney, draw readers straight into the world of Arnold Spirit.... Junior's honest, critical eye and verbal succinctness give this story a verve and humor that make it irresistible.... This is utterly engaging as a teen novel. For many, it will open up a new world of awareness."　　　　　　—**TORONTO STAR SUNDAY**

"Often outrageous comics accompany often X-rated narrative; both are sweet and cynical, hilarious and brutally honest, tender and achingly sad."
　　　　　　　　　　　　—SAN FRANCISCO CHRONICLE

"In his first work of fiction for young adults, [Sherman Alexie] has created an endearing teen protagonist in his own likeness and placed him in the here and now."
　　　　　　　　　　　—MINNEAPOLIS STAR TRIBUNE

The Absolutely True Diary of a Part-Time Indian

10th Anniversary Edition

by Sherman Alexie

Art by Ellen Forney

Foreword by Jacqueline Woodson

Little, Brown and Company

New York · Boston

Little, Brown and Company
Hachette Book Group
1290 Avenue of the Americas, New York, NY 10104
Visit us at LBYR.com

Originally published in hardcover and ebook by Little, Brown and Company in September 2007
First Tenth-Anniversary Edition: September 2017

Little, Brown and Company is a division of Hachette Book Group, Inc. The Little, Brown name and logo are trademarks of Hachette Book Group, Inc.

The publisher is not responsible for websites (or their content) that are not owned by the publisher.

The Library of Congress has cataloged the original edition as follows:
Alexie, Sherman, 1966–
The absolutely true diary of a part-time Indian / by Sherman Alexie ; art by Ellen Forney.
p. cm.
Summary: Budding cartoonist Junior leaves his troubled school on the Spokane Indian Reservation to attend an all-white farm town school where the only other Indian is the school mascot.
HC ISBN 978-0-316-01368-0 / PB ISBN 978-0-316-01369-7
1. Spokane Indians—Juvenile fiction. [1. Spokane Indians—Fiction. 2. Indians of North America—Washington (State)—Fiction. 3. Indian reservations—Fiction. 4. Race relations—Fiction. 5. Diaries—Fiction.] I. Forney, Ellen, ill. II. Title.
PZ7.A382Ab 2007
[Fic]—dc22
2007022799

ISBNs: 978-0-316-50404-1 (tenth anniversary), 978-0-316-43988-6 (large print), 978-0-316-21930-3 (ebook)

Printed in the United States of America
LSC-C
10 9 8 7 6 5 4 3 2 1

For Wellpinit
and
Reardan,
my hometowns

Foreword

"I was born with water on the brain." The opening line from a masterful work by a genius storyteller. The other night I thought I'd try reading this book out loud to my nine-year-old son. The copy we have is worn and dog-eared, a first edition bought only a few days after it was published in 2007. At the time I didn't yet have a son, and my daughter was still very young. I had bought Sherman Alexie's *The Absolutely True Diary of a Part-Time Indian* for myself, having already, before it was published, heard how amazing it was. With that opening line, Alexie brought me into the world of Junior—struggling artist, ballplayer, survivor of two very different kinds of education. And inside Junior's world, I was awakened to life on the reservation—meeting people and finding myself in situations I had never imagined.

Dr. Rudine Sims Bishop, who has written extensively about the importance of children's literature, talks about how books can be both mirrors and windows—mirrors in which readers can see themselves on the pages of literature and thereby know their existence in the world is valid and true, and windows into worlds they might never have imagined. This book is a window into Junior's world—a window Alexie pulls the curtains back from and lovingly invites us into. But it is also a mirror for the many First Nations people who have not seen themselves in literature. It is hard to read *The Absolutely True Diary of a Part-Time Indian* and not find a part of yourself in its pages.

The other night, as my son and I ascended the stairs to his bedroom, I grabbed the book off the shelf—"Let's just try it," I said. My son, holding a comic book, said, "No." Flatly. "Yes," I said. "We're going to give it a try." I knew at once he'd love Junior and Rowdy and the many people he'd meet on the reservation. With that first line, my boy was hooked, the way I had been many years ago. The way my now-teenage daughter had been two summers ago, when she closed the book and exclaimed, "This book is *so* good, I can*not* believe it was assigned."

How does one author touch so many different people at so many different points in their lives? Alexie's brilliance lies in his ability to speak truth to power with humor, grace, and love. He loves the characters he brings to the page, and, by extension, we fall in love with them, too. Two pages in, I told my son we could move on to his comic book if he wanted. "Nah," he said. "Keep reading." After a moment, he smiled and said, "I think this book is going to be good."

We read long past his bedtime. For me, moving back into Junior's world felt like visiting an old friend. For my son and for so many of you coming to this story for the first time, I know this book will be revisited often and, most of all, loved deeply.

—Jacqueline Woodson

There is
another world,
but it is in this one.
W.B. Yeats

The Black-
Eye-of-
the-Month
Club
✳

I was born with water on the brain.

Okay, so that's not exactly true. I was actually born with too much cerebral spinal fluid inside my skull. But cerebral spinal fluid is just the doctors' fancy way of saying brain grease. And brain grease works inside the lobes like car grease works inside an engine. It keeps things running smooth and fast. But weirdo me, I was born with too much grease inside my skull, and it got all thick and muddy and disgusting, and it only mucked up the works. My thinking and breathing and living engine slowed down and flooded.

My brain was drowning in grease.

But that makes the whole thing sound weirdo and funny, like my brain was a giant French fry, so it seems more serious and poetic and accurate to say, "I was born with water on the brain."

Okay, so maybe that's not a very serious way to say it, either. Maybe the whole thing *is* weird and funny.

But jeez, did my mother and father and big sister and grandma and cousins and aunts and uncles think it was funny when the doctors cut open my little skull and sucked out all that extra water with some tiny vacuum?

I was only six months old and I was supposed to croak during the surgery. And even if I somehow survived the mini-Hoover, I was supposed to suffer serious brain damage during the procedure and live the rest of my life as a vegetable.

Well, I obviously survived the surgery. I wouldn't be writing this if I didn't, but I have all sorts of physical problems that are directly the result of my brain damage.

First of all, I ended up having forty-two teeth. The typical human has thirty-two, right? But I had forty-two.

Ten more than usual.

Ten more than normal.

Ten teeth past human.

My teeth got so crowded that I could barely close my mouth. I went to Indian Health Service to get some teeth pulled so I could eat normally, not like some slobbering vulture. But the Indian Health Service funded major dental work only once a year, so I had to have all ten extra teeth pulled *in one day*.

And what's more, our white dentist believed that Indians only felt half as much pain as white people did, so he only gave us half the Novocain.

What a bastard, huh?

Indian Health Service also funded eyeglass purchases only once a year and offered one style: those ugly, thick, black plastic ones.

My brain damage left me nearsighted in one eye and farsighted in the other, so my ugly glasses were all lopsided because my eyes were so lopsided.

I get headaches because my eyes are, like, enemies, you know, like they used to be married to each other but now hate each other's guts.

And I started wearing glasses when I was three, so I ran around the rez looking like a three-year-old Indian *grandpa*.

And, oh, I was skinny. I'd turn sideways and *disappear*.

But my hands and feet were huge. My feet were a size eleven in third grade! With my big feet and pencil body, I looked like a capital *L* walking down the road.

And my skull was enormous.

Epic.

My head was so big that little Indian skulls orbited around it. Some of the kids called me Orbit. And other kids just called me Globe. The bullies would pick me up, spin me in circles, put their finger down on my skull, and say, "I want to go there."

So obviously, I looked goofy on the outside, but it was the *inside* stuff that was the worst.

First of all, I had seizures. At least two a week. So I was damaging my brain on a regular basis. But the thing is, I was having those seizures because I *already* had brain damage, so I was reopening wounds each time I seized.

Yep, whenever I had a seizure, I was *damaging my damage*.

I haven't had a seizure in seven years, but the doctors tell me that I am "susceptible to seizure activity."

Susceptible to seizure activity.

Doesn't that just roll off the tongue like poetry?

I also had a stutter and a lisp. Or maybe I should say I had a st-st-st-st-stutter and a lisssssssththththp.

You wouldn't think there is anything life threatening about speech impediments, but let me tell you, there is nothing more dangerous than being a kid with a stutter and a lisp.

A five-year-old is cute when he lisps and stutters. Heck, most of the big-time kid actors stuttered and lisped their way to stardom.

And jeez, you're still fairly cute when you're a stuttering and lisping six-, seven-, and eight-year-old, but it's all over when you turn nine and ten.

After that, your stutter and lisp turn you into a retard.

And if you're fourteen years old, like me, and you're still stuttering and lisping, then you become the biggest retard in the world.

Everybody on the rez calls me a retard about twice a day. They call me retard when they are pantsing me or stuffing my head in the toilet or just smacking me upside the head.

I'm not even writing down this story the way I actually talk, because I'd have to fill it with stutters and lisps, and then you'd be wondering why you're reading a story written by *such a retard.*

Do you know what happens to retards on the rez?

We get beat up.

At least once a month.

Yep, I belong to the Black-Eye-of-the-Month Club.

Sure I want to go outside. Every kid wants to go outside. But it's safer to stay at home. So I mostly hang out alone in my bedroom and read books and draw cartoons.

Here's one of me:

I draw all the time.

I draw cartoons of my mother and father; my sister and grandmother; my best friend, Rowdy; and everybody else on the rez.

I draw because words are too unpredictable.

I draw because words are too limited.

If you speak and write in English, or Spanish, or Chinese, or any other language, then only a certain percentage of human beings will get your meaning.

But when you draw a picture, everybody can understand it.

If I draw a cartoon of a flower, then every man, woman, and child in the world can look at it and say, "That's a flower."

So I draw because I want to talk to the world. And I want the world to pay attention to me.

I feel important with a pen in my hand. I feel like I might grow up to be somebody important. An artist. Maybe a famous artist. Maybe a rich artist.

That's the only way I can become rich and famous.

Just take a look at the world. Almost all of the rich and famous brown people are artists. They're singers and actors and writers and dancers and directors and poets.

So I draw because I feel like it might be my only real chance to escape the reservation.

I think the world is a series of broken dams and floods, and my cartoons are tiny little lifeboats.

Why Chicken
Means So
Much to Me
✳

Okay, so now you know that I'm a cartoonist. And I think I'm pretty good at it, too. But no matter how good I am, my cartoons will never take the place of food or money. I wish I could draw a peanut butter and jelly sandwich, or a fist full of twenty dollar bills, and perform some magic trick and make it real. But I can't do that. Nobody can do that, not even the hungriest magician in the world.

· I wish I were magical, but I am really just a poor-ass reservation kid living with his poor-ass family on the poor-ass Spokane Indian Reservation.

Do you know the worst thing about being poor? Oh, maybe you've done the math in your head and you figure:

Poverty = empty refrigerator + empty stomach

And sure, sometimes, my family misses a meal, and sleep is the only thing we have for dinner, but I know that, sooner or later, my parents will come bursting through the door with a bucket of Kentucky Fried Chicken.

Original Recipe.

And hey, in a weird way, being hungry makes food taste better. There is nothing better than a chicken leg when you haven't eaten for (approximately) eighteen-and-a-half hours. And believe me, a good piece of chicken can make anybody believe in the existence of God.

← the Shroud of Kentucky Fried

So hunger is not the worst thing about being poor.

And now I'm sure you're asking, "Okay, okay, Mr. Hunger Artist, Mr. Mouth-Full-of-Words, Mr. Woe-Is-Me, Mr. Secret Recipe, what is the worst thing about being poor?"

So, okay, I'll tell you the worst thing.

Last week, my best friend Oscar got really sick.

At first, I thought he just had heat exhaustion or something. I mean, it was a crazy-hot July day (102 degrees with 90 percent humidity), and plenty of people were falling over from heat exhaustion, so why not a little dog wearing a fur coat?

I tried to give him some water, but he didn't want any of that.

He was lying on his bed with red, watery, snotty eyes. He whimpered in pain. When I touched him, he yelped like crazy.

It was like his nerves were poking out three inches from his skin.

I figured he'd be okay with some rest, but then he started vomiting, and diarrhea blasted out of him, and he had these seizures where his little legs just kicked and kicked and kicked.

And sure, Oscar was only an adopted stray mutt, but he was the only living thing that I could depend on. He was more dependable than my parents, grandmother, aunts, uncles, cousins, and big sister. He taught me more than any teachers ever did.

Honestly, Oscar was a better person than any human I had ever known.

"Mom," I said. "We have to take Oscar to the vet."

"He'll be all right," she said.

But she was *lying*. Her eyes always got darker in the middle when she lied. She was a Spokane Indian and a bad liar, which didn't make any sense. We Indians really should be better liars, considering how often we've been lied to.

"He's really sick, Mom," I said. "He's going to die if we don't take him to the doctor."

She looked hard at me. And her eyes weren't dark anymore, so I knew that she was going to tell me the truth. And trust me, there are times when the *last thing* you want to hear is the truth.

"Junior, sweetheart," Mom said. "I'm sorry, but we don't have any money for Oscar."

"I'll pay you back," I said. "I promise."

"Honey, it'll cost hundreds of dollars, maybe a thousand."

"I'll pay back the doctor. I'll get a job."

Mom smiled all sad and hugged me hard.

Jeez, how stupid was I? What kind of job can a reservation Indian boy get? I was too young to deal blackjack at the casino, there were only about fifteen green grass lawns on the reservation (and none of their owners outsourced the mowing jobs), and the only paper route was owned by a tribal elder named Wally. And he had to deliver only fifty papers, so his job was more like a hobby.

There was nothing I could do to save Oscar.

Nothing.

Nothing.

Nothing.

So I lay down on the floor beside him and patted his head and whispered his name *for hours*.

Then Dad came home from *wherever* and had one of those long talks with Mom, and they decided something *without me*.

And then Dad pulled down his rifle and bullets from the closet.

"Junior," he said. "Carry Oscar outside."

"No!" I screamed.

"He's suffering," Dad said. "We have to help him."

"You can't do it!" I shouted.

I wanted to punch my dad in the face. I wanted to punch him in the nose and make him bleed. I wanted to punch him in the eye and make him blind. I wanted to kick him in the balls and make him pass out.

I was hot mad. Volcano mad. Tsunami mad.

Dad just looked down at me with the saddest look in his eyes. He was crying. He looked *weak*.

I wanted to hate him for his weakness.

I wanted to hate Dad and Mom for our poverty.

I wanted to blame them for my sick dog and for all the other sickness in the world.

But I can't blame my parents for our poverty because my mother and father are the twin suns around which I orbit and my world would EXPLODE without them.

And it's not like my mother and father were born into wealth. It's not like they gambled away their family fortunes. My parents came from poor people who came from poor people who came from poor people, all the way back to the very first poor people.

Adam and Eve covered their privates with fig leaves; the first Indians covered their privates *with their tiny hands*.

Seriously, I know my mother and father had their dreams when they were kids. They dreamed about being something other than poor, but they never got the chance to be anything because nobody paid attention to their dreams.

Given the chance, my mother would have gone to college.

She still reads books like crazy. She buys them by the pound. And she remembers everything she reads. She can

recite whole pages by memory. She's a human tape recorder. Really, my mom can read the newspaper in fifteen minutes and tell me baseball scores, the location of every war, the latest guy to win the Lottery, and the high temperature in Des Moines, Iowa.

Given the chance, my father would have been a musician.

When he gets drunk, he sings old country songs. And blues, too. And he sounds good. Like a pro. Like he should be on the radio. He plays the guitar and the piano a little bit. And he has this old saxophone from high school that he keeps all clean and shiny, like he's going to join a band at any moment.

But we reservation Indians don't get to realize our dreams. We don't get those chances. Or choices. We're just poor. That's all we are.

It sucks to be poor, and it sucks to feel that you somehow *deserve* to be poor. You start believing that you're poor because you're stupid and ugly. And then you start believing that you're stupid and ugly because you're Indian. And because you're Indian you start believing you're destined to be poor. It's an ugly circle and *there's nothing you can do about it.*

Poverty doesn't give you strength or teach you lessons about perseverance. No, poverty only teaches you how to be poor.

So, poor and small and weak, I picked up Oscar. He licked my face because he loved and trusted me. And I carried him out to the lawn, and I laid him down beneath our green apple tree.

"I love you, Oscar," I said.

He looked at me and I swear to you that he understood what was happening. He knew what Dad was going to do. But Oscar wasn't scared. He was relieved.

But not me.

I ran away from there as fast as I could.

I wanted to run faster than the speed of sound, but nobody, no matter how much pain they're in, can run that fast. So I heard the boom of my father's rifle when he shot my best friend.

A bullet only costs about two cents, and anybody can afford that.

Revenge Is
My Middle
Name
✹

After Oscar died, I was so depressed that I thought about crawling into a hole and disappearing forever.

But Rowdy talked me out of it.

"It's not like anybody's going to notice if you go away," he said. "So you might as well gut it out."

Isn't that tough love?

Rowdy is the toughest kid on the rez. He is long and lean and strong like a snake.

His heart is as strong and mean as a snake, too.

But he is my best human friend and he cares about me, so he would always tell me the truth.

And he is right. Nobody would miss me if I was gone.

Well, Rowdy would miss me, but he'd never admit that he'd miss me. He is way too tough for that kind of emotion.

But aside from Rowdy, and my parents and sister and grandmother, nobody would miss me.

I am a zero on the rez. And if you subtract zero from zero, you still have zero. So what's the point of subtracting when the answer is always the same?

So I gut it out.

I have to, I guess, especially since Rowdy is having one of the worst summers of his life.

His father is drinking hard and throwing hard punches, so Rowdy and his mother are always walking around with bruised and bloody faces.

"It's war paint," Rowdy always says. "It just makes me look tougher."

And I suppose it does make him look tougher, because Rowdy never tries to hide his wounds. He walks around the rez with a black eye and split lip.

This morning, he limped into our house, slumped in a chair, threw his sprained knee up on the table, and smirked.

He had a bandage over his left ear.

"What happened to your head?" I asked.

"Dad said I wasn't listening," Rowdy said. "So he got all drunk and tried to make my ear a little bigger."

My mother and father are drunks, too, but they aren't mean like that. Not at all. They sometimes ignore me. Sometimes they yell at me. But they never, ever, never, ever hit me. I've never even been spanked. Really. I think my mother sometimes wants to haul off and give me a slap, but my father won't let it happen.

He doesn't believe in physical punishment; he believes in staring so cold at me that I turn into a ice-covered ice cube with an icy filling.

My house is a safe place, so Rowdy spends most of his time with us. It's like he's a family member, an extra brother and son.

"You want to head down to the powwow?" Rowdy asked.

"Nah," I said.

The Spokane Tribe holds their annual powwow celebration over the Labor Day weekend. This was the 127th annual one, and there would be singing, war dancing, gambling, storytelling, laughter, fry bread, hamburgers, hot dogs, arts and crafts, and plenty of alcoholic brawling.

I wanted no part of it.

Oh, the dancing and singing are great. Beautiful, in fact, but I'm afraid of all the Indians who aren't dancers and singers. Those rhythmless, talentless, tuneless Indians are most likely going to get drunk and beat the shit out of any available losers.

And I am always the most available loser.

"Come on," Rowdy said. "I'll protect you."

He knew that I was afraid of getting beat up. And he also knew that he'd probably have to fight for me.

Rowdy has protected me since we were born.

Both of us were pushed into the world on November 5, 1992, at Sacred Heart Hospital in Spokane. I'm two hours older than Rowdy. I was born all broken and twisted, and he was born mad.

He was always crying and screaming and kicking and punching.

He bit his mother's breast when she tried to nurse him. He kept biting her, so she gave up and fed him formula.

He really hasn't changed much since then.

Well, at fourteen years old, it's not like he runs around biting women's breasts, but he does punch and kick and spit.

He got into his first fistfight in kindergarten. He took on three first graders during a snowball fight because one of them had thrown a piece of ice. Rowdy punched them out pretty quickly.

And then he punched the teacher who came to stop the fight.

He didn't hurt the teacher, not at all, but man, let me tell you, that teacher was angry.

"What's wrong with you?" he yelled.

"Everything!" Rowdy yelled back.

Rowdy fought everybody.

He fought boys and girls.

Men and women.

He fought stray dogs.

Hell, he fought the weather.

He'd throw wild punches at rain.

Honestly.

"Come on, you wuss," Rowdy said. "Let's go to powwow. You can't hide in your house forever. You'll turn into some kind of troll or something."

"What if somebody picks on me?" I asked.

"Then I'll pick on them."

"What if somebody picks my nose?" I asked.

"Then I'll pick your nose, too," Rowdy said.

"You're my hero," I said.

"Come to the powwow," Rowdy said. "Please."

It's a big deal when Rowdy is polite.

"Okay, okay," I said.

So Rowdy and I walked the three miles to the powwow grounds. It was dark, maybe eight o'clock or so, and the drummers and singers were loud and wonderful.

I was excited. But I was getting hypothermic, too.

The Spokane Powwow is wicked hot during the day and freezing cold at night.

"I should have worn my coat," I said.

"Toughen up," Rowdy said.

"Let's go watch the chicken dancers," I said.

I think the chicken dancers are cool because, well, they dance like chickens. And you already know how much I love chicken.

"This crap is boring," Rowdy said.

"We'll just watch for a little while," I said. "And then we'll go gamble or something."

"Okay," Rowdy said. He is the only person who listens to me.

We weaved our way through the parked cars, vans, SUVs, RVs, plastic tents, and deer-hide tepees.

"Hey, let's go buy some bootleg whiskey," Rowdy said. "I got five bucks."

"Don't get drunk," I said. "You'll just get ugly."

"I'm already ugly," Rowdy said.

He laughed, tripped over a tent pole, and stumbled into a minivan. He bumped his face against a window and jammed his shoulder against the rearview mirror.

It was pretty funny, so I laughed.

That was a mistake.

Rowdy got mad.

He shoved me to the ground and almost kicked me. He swung his leg at me, but pulled it back at the last second. I could tell he wanted to hurt me for laughing. But I am his friend, his best friend, his only friend. He couldn't hurt me. So he grabbed a garbage sack filled with empty beer bottles and hucked it at the minivan.

Glass broke everywhere.

Then Rowdy grabbed a shovel that somebody had been using to dig barbecue holes and went after that van. Just beat the crap out of it.

Smash! Boom! Bam!

He dented the doors and smashed the windows and knocked off the mirrors.

I was scared of Rowdy and I was scared of getting thrown in jail for vandalism, so I ran.

That was a mistake.

I ran right into the Andruss brothers' camp. The Andrusses — John, Jim, and Joe — are the cruelest triplets in the history of the world.

"Hey, look," one of them said. "It's Hydro Head."

Yep, those bastards were making fun of my brain disorder. Charming, huh?

"Nah, he ain't Hydro," said another one of the brothers. "He's Hydrogen."

I don't know which one said that. I couldn't tell them apart. I decided to run again, but one of them grabbed me, and shoved me toward another brother. All three of them shoved me to and fro. They were playing catch with me.

"Hydromatic."

"Hydrocarbon."

"Hydrocrack."

"Hydrodynamic."

"Hydroelectric."

"Hydro-and-Low."

"Hydro-and-Seek."

I fell down. One of the brothers picked me up, dusted me off, and then kneed me in the balls.

I fell down again, holding my tender crotch, and tried not to scream.

The Andruss brothers laughed and walked away.

Oh, by the way, did I mention that the Andruss triplets are thirty years old?

What kind of men beat up a fourteen-year-old boy?

Major-league assholes.

I was lying on the ground, holding my nuts as tenderly as a squirrel holds his nuts, when Rowdy walked up.

"Who did this to you?" he asked.

"The Andruss brothers," I said.

"Did they hit you in the head?" Rowdy asked. He knows that my brain is fragile. If those Andruss brothers had punched a hole in the aquarium of my skull, I might have flooded out the entire powwow.

"My brain is fine," I said. "But my balls are dying."

"I'm going to kill those bastards," Rowdy said.

Of course, Rowdy didn't kill them, but we hid near the Andruss brothers' camp until three in the morning. They staggered back and passed out in their tent. Then Rowdy snuck in, shaved off their eyebrows, and cut off their braids.

That's about the worst thing you can do to an Indian guy. It had taken them years to grow their hair. And Rowdy cut that away in five seconds.

I loved Rowdy for doing that. I felt guilty for loving him for that. But revenge also feels pretty good.

The Andruss brothers never did figure out who cut their eyebrows and hair. Rowdy started a rumor that it was a bunch of Makah Indians from the coast who did it.

"You can't trust them whale hunters," Rowdy said. "They'll do anything."

But before you think Rowdy is only good for revenge, and kicking the shit out of minivans, raindrops, and people, let me tell you something sweet about him: he loves comic books.

But not the cool superhero ones like *Daredevil* or *X-Men*. No, he reads the goofy old ones, like *Richie Rich* and *Archie* and *Casper the Friendly Ghost*. Kid stuff. He keeps them hidden in a hole in the wall of his bedroom closet. Almost every day, I'll head over to his house and we'll read those comics together.

Rowdy isn't a fast reader, but he's persistent. And he'll just laugh and laugh at the dumb jokes, no matter how many times he's read the same comic.

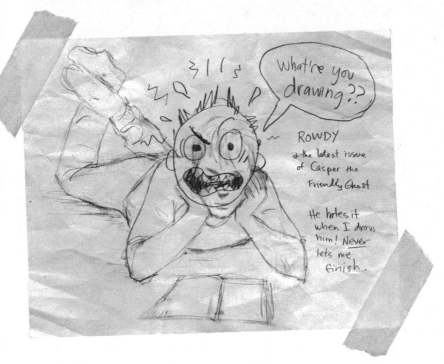

I like the sound of Rowdy's laughter. I don't hear it very often, but it's always sort of this avalanche of ha-ha and ho-ho and hee-hee.

I like to make him laugh. He loves my cartoons.

He's a big, goofy dreamer, too, just like me. He likes to pretend he lives inside the comic books. I guess a fake life inside a cartoon is a lot better than his real life.

So I draw cartoons to make him happy, to give him other worlds to live inside.

I draw his dreams.

And he only talks about his dreams with me. And I only talk about my dreams with him.

I tell him about my fears.

I think Rowdy might be the most important person in my life. Maybe more important than my family. Can your best friend be more important than your family?

I think so.

I mean, after all, I spend a lot more time with Rowdy than I do with anyone else.

Let's do the math.

I figure Rowdy and I have spent an average of eight hours a day together for the last fourteen years.

That's eight hours times 365 days times fourteen years.

So that means Rowdy and I have spent 40,880 hours in each other's company.

Nobody else comes anywhere close to that.

Trust me.

Rowdy and I are inseparable.

Because
Geometry
Is Not a
Country
Somewhere
Near France
✳

I was fourteen and it was my first day of high school. I was happy about that. And I was most especially excited about my first geometry class.

Yep, I have to admit that isosceles triangles make me feel *hormonal.*

Most guys, no matter what age, get excited about curves and circles, but not me. Don't get me wrong. I like girls and their curves. And I really like women and their curvier curves.

I spend *hours* in the bathroom with a magazine that has one thousand pictures of naked movie stars:

Naked woman + right hand = happy happy joy joy

Yep, that's right, I admit that I masturbate.

I'm proud of it.

I'm good at it.

I'm ambidextrous.

If there were a Professional Masturbators League, I'd get drafted number one and make millions of dollars.

And maybe you're thinking, "Well, you really shouldn't be talking about masturbation in public."

Well, tough, I'm going to talk about it because EVERY-BODY does it. And EVERYBODY likes it.

And if God hadn't wanted us to masturbate, then God wouldn't have given us thumbs.

So I thank God for my thumbs.

But, the thing is, no matter how much time my thumbs and I spend with the curves of imaginary women, I am much more in love with the right angles of buildings.

When I was a baby, I'd crawl under my bed and snuggle into a corner to sleep. I just felt warm and safe leaning into two walls at the same time.

When I was eight, nine, and ten, I slept in my bedroom closet with the door closed. I only stopped doing that because my big sister, Mary, told me that I was just trying to find my way back into my mother's womb.

That ruined the whole closet thing.

Don't get me wrong. I don't have anything against my mother's womb. I was built in there, after all. So I have to say that I am pro-womb. But I have zero interest in moving back home, so to speak.

My sister is good at ruining things.

After high school, my sister just froze. Didn't go to college, didn't get a job. Didn't do anything. Kind of sad, I guess.

THE ABSOLUTELY TRUE DIARY OF A PART-TIME INDIAN

MARY RUNS AWAY

looks like Jennifer Lopez (if J. Lo was smarter)

acne scars that somehow make her look tough & pretty at the same time

lightning-bolt tattoo on the back of her neck

tie-dyed T-shirt (shoplifted from The Gap)

"distressed" blue jeans (shoplifted from Macy's)

Birkenstock sandals (stolen from the feet of an unconscious white pot dealer and poet)

But she is also beautiful and strong and funny. She is the prettiest and strongest and funniest person who ever spent twenty-three hours a day alone in a basement.

She is so crazy and random that we call her Mary Runs Away. I'm not like her at all. I am steady. I'm excited about life.

I'm excited about school.

Rowdy and I are planning on playing high school basketball.

Last year, Rowdy and I were the best players on the eighth-grade team. But I don't think I'll be a very good high school player.

Rowdy is probably going to start varsity as a freshman, but I figure the bigger and better kids will crush me. It's one thing to hit jumpers over other eighth graders; it's a whole other thing to score on high school monsters.

I'll probably be a benchwarmer on the C squad while Rowdy goes on to all-state glory and fame.

I am a little worried that Rowdy will start to hang around with the older guys and leave me behind.

I'm also worried that he'll start to pick on me, too.

I'm scared he might start hating me as much as all of the others do.

But I am more happy than scared.

And I know that the other kids are going to give me crap for being so excited about school. But I don't care.

I was sitting in a freshman classroom at Wellpinit High School when Mr. P strolled in with a box full of geometry textbooks.

And let me tell you, Mr. P is a weird-looking dude.

But no matter how weird he looks, the absolutely weirdest thing about Mr. P is that sometimes he *forgets* to come to school.

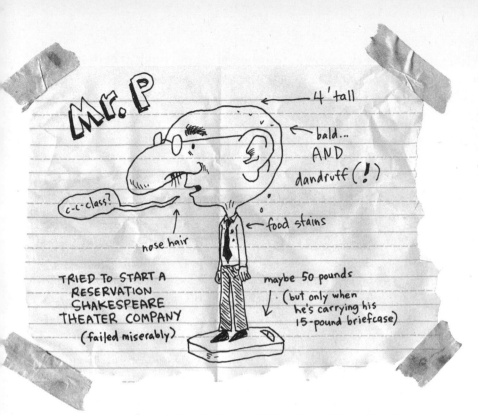

Mr. P

4' tall

bald...
AND
dandruff (!)

c-c-class?

nose hair

food stains

TRIED TO START A
RESERVATION
SHAKESPEARE
THEATER COMPANY
(failed miserably)

maybe 50 pounds
(but only when
he's carrying his
15-pound briefcase)

Let me repeat that: MR. P SOMETIMES FORGETS TO COME TO SCHOOL!

Yep, we have to send a kid down to the teachers' housing compound behind the school to wake Mr. P, who is always conking out in front of his TV.

That's right. Mr. P sometimes teaches class in his *pajamas.*

He is a weird old coot, but most of the kids dig him because he doesn't ask too much of us. I mean, how can you expect your students to work hard if you show up in your pajamas *and slippers*?

And yeah, I know it's weird, but the tribe actually houses all of the teachers in one-bedroom cottages and musty, old trailer houses behind the school. You can't teach at our school if you don't live in the compound. It was like some kind of prison-work farm for our liberal, white, vegetarian do-gooders and conservative, white missionary saviors.

Some of our teachers make us eat birdseed so we'll feel closer to the earth, and other teachers hate birds because they are supposedly minions of the Devil. It is like being taught by Jekyll and Hyde.

But Mr. P isn't a Democratic-, Republican-, Christian-, or Devil-worshipping freak. He is just *sleepy*.

But some folks are absolutely convinced he is, like, this Sicilian accountant who testified against the Mafia, and had to be hidden by that secret Witness Relocation Program.

It makes some goofy sort of sense, I suppose.

If the government wants to hide somebody, there's probably no place more isolated than my reservation, which is located approximately one million miles north of Important and two billion miles west of Happy. But jeez, I think people pay way too much attention to *The Sopranos*.

Mostly, I just think Mr. P is a lonely old man who used to be a lonely young man. And for some reason I don't understand, lonely white people love to hang around lonelier Indians.

"All right, kids, let's get cracking," Mr. P said as he passed out the geometry books. "How about we do something strange and start on page one?"

I grabbed my book and opened it up.

I wanted to smell it.

Heck, I wanted to kiss it.

Yes, kiss it.

That's right, I am a book kisser.

Maybe that's kind of perverted or maybe it's just romantic and highly *intelligent*.

But my lips and I stopped short when I saw this written on the inside front cover:

This Book Belongs to Agnes Adams

Okay, now you're probably asking yourself, "Who is Agnes Adams?"

Well, let me tell you. Agnes Adams is my mother. MY MOTHER! And Adams is her *maiden* name.

So that means my mother was born an Adams and she was still an Adams when she wrote her name in that book. And she was thirty when she gave birth to me. Yep, so that means I was staring at a geometry book that was at least thirty years older than I was.

I couldn't believe it.

How horrible is that?

My school and my tribe are so poor and sad that we have to study from the same dang books our parents studied from. That is absolutely the saddest thing in the world.

And let me tell you, that old, old, old, *decrepit* geometry book hit my heart with the force of a nuclear bomb. My hopes and dreams floated up in a mushroom cloud. What do you do when the world has declared nuclear war on you?

Hope Against Hope ✻

Of course, I was suspended from school after I smashed Mr. P in the face, even though it was a complete accident.

Okay, so it wasn't exactly an accident.

After all, I wanted to hit *something* when I threw that ancient book. But I didn't want to hit *somebody,* and I certainly didn't plan on breaking the nose of a mafioso math teacher.

"That's the first time you've ever hit anything you aimed at," my big sister said.

"We are so disappointed," my mother said.

"We are so disappointed *in you,*" my father said.

My grandmother just sat in her rocking chair and cried and cried.

I was ashamed. I'd never really been in trouble before.

A week into my suspension, I was sitting on our front porch, thinking about stuff, *contemplating*, when old Mr. P walked up our driveway. He had a big bandage on his face.

"I'm sorry about your face," I said.

"I'm sorry they suspended you," he said. "I hope you know that wasn't my idea."

After I smashed him in the face, I figured Mr. P wanted to hire a hit man. Well, maybe that's taking it too far. Mr. P didn't want me dead, but I don't think he would have minded if I'd been the only survivor of a plane that crashed into the Pacific Ocean.

At the very least, I thought they were going to send me to jail.

"Can I sit down with you?" Mr. P asked.

"You bet," I said. I was nervous. Why was he being so friendly? Was he planning a sneak attack on me? Maybe he was going to smash me in the nose with a calculus book.

But the old guy just sat in peaceful silence for a long time.

I didn't know what to do or say, so I just sat as quietly as he did. That silence got so big and real that it felt like three people sat on the porch.

"Do you know why you hit me with that book?" Mr. P finally asked.

It was a trick question. I knew I needed to answer correctly or he'd be mad.

"I hit you because I'm stupid."

"You're not stupid."

Wrong answer.

Shoot.

I tried again.

"I didn't mean to hit you," I said. "I was aiming for the wall."

"Were you really aiming for the wall?"

Dang it.

He was, like, *interrogating* me.

I was starting to get *upset*.

"No," I said. "I wasn't aiming for anything really. Well, I was planning on hitting something, you know? Like the wall or a desk or the chalkboard. Something dead, you know, not something alive."

"Alive like me?"

"Or like a plant."

Mr. P had three plants in his classroom. He talked to those green things more often than he talked to us.

"You do know that hitting a plant and hitting me are two different things, right?" he asked.

"Yeah, I know."

He smiled mysteriously. Adults are so good at smiling mysteriously. Do they go to college for that?

I was getting more and more freaked out. What did he want?

"You know, Mr. P, I don't mean to be rude or anything, but you're, like, freaking me out here. I mean, why are you here, exactly?"

"Well, I want you to know that hitting me with that book was probably the worst thing you've ever done. It doesn't matter what you intended to do. What happens is what you really did. And you broke an old man's nose. That's almost unforgivable."

He was going to punish me now. He couldn't beat me up with his old man fists, but he could hurt me with his old man words.

"But I do forgive you," he said. "No matter how much I don't want to. I have to forgive you. It's the only thing that keeps me from smacking you with an ugly stick. When I first started teaching here, that's what we did to the rowdy ones, you know? We beat them. That's how we were taught to teach you. We were supposed to kill the Indian to save the child."

"You *killed* Indians?"

"No, no, it's just a saying. I didn't literally kill Indians. We were supposed to make you give up being Indian. Your songs and stories and language and dancing. Everything. We weren't trying to kill Indian people. We were trying to kill Indian culture."

Man, at that second, I hated Mr. P *hard*. I wished I had a whole dang set of encyclopedias to throw at him.

"I can't apologize to everybody I hurt," Mr. P said. "But I can apologize to you."

It was so backward. I'd broken *his* nose but he was trying to apologize *to me*.

"I hurt a lot of Indian kids when I was a young teacher," he said. "I might have broken a few bones."

All of a sudden, I realized he was *confessing* to me.

"It was a different time," Mr. P said. "A bad time. Very bad. It was wrong. But I was young and stupid and full of ideas. Just like you."

Mr. P smiled. He smiled at me. There was a piece of lettuce stuck between his front teeth.

"You know," he said. "I taught your sister, too."

"I know."

"She was the smartest kid I ever had. She was even smarter than you."

I knew my sister was smart. But I'd never heard a teacher say that about her. And I'd never heard anybody say that she was smarter than me. I was happy and jealous at the same time.

My sister, the basement mole rat, was smarter than me?

"Well," I said, "My mom and dad are pretty smart, too, so I guess it runs in the family."

"Your sister wanted to be a writer," Mr. P said.

"Really?" I asked.

I was surprised by that. She'd never said anything about that to me. Or to Mom and Dad. Or to anybody.

"I never heard her say that," I said.

"She was shy about it," Mr. P said. "She always thought people would make fun of her."

"For writing books? People would have thought she was a hero around here. Maybe she could have made movies or something, too. That would have been cool."

"Well, she wasn't shy about the idea of writing books. She was shy about the kind of books she wanted to write."

"What kind of books did she want to write?" I asked.

"You're going to laugh."

"No, I'm not."

"Yes, you are."

"No, I'm not."

"Yes, you are."

Jeez, we had both turned into seven-year-olds.

"Just tell me," I said.

It was weird that a teacher was telling me things I didn't know about my sister. It made me wonder what else I didn't know about her.

"She wanted to write romance novels."

Of course, I giggled at that idea.

"Hey," Mr. P said. "You weren't supposed to laugh."

"I didn't laugh."

"Yes, you laughed."

"No, I didn't."

"Yes, you did."

"Maybe I laughed a little."

"A little laugh is still a laugh."

And then I laughed for real. A big laugh.

"Romance novels," I said. "Those things are just sort of silly, aren't they?"

"Lots of people — mostly women — love them," Mr. P said. "They buy millions of them. There are lots of writers who make millions by writing romance novels."

"What kind of romances?" I asked.

"She never really said, but she did like to read the Indian ones. You know the ones I'm talking about?"

Yes, I did know. Those romances always featured a love affair between a virginal white schoolteacher or preacher's wife and a half-breed Indian warrior. The covers were hilarious:

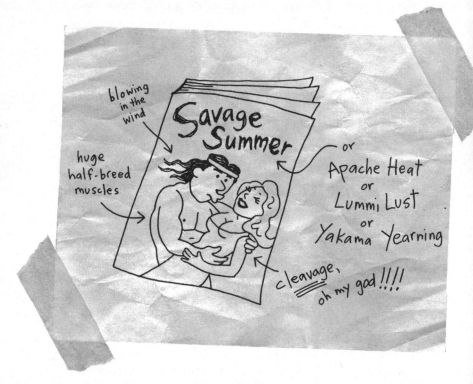

"You know," I said, "I don't think I ever saw my sister reading one of those things."

"She kept them hidden," Mr. P said.

Well, that is a big difference between my sister and me. I hide the magazines filled with photos of naked women; my sister hides her tender romance novels that tell stories about naked women (and men).

I want the pictures; my sister wants the words.

"I don't remember her ever writing anything," I said.

"Oh, she loved to write short stories. Little romantic stories. She wouldn't let anybody read them. But she'd always be scribbling in her notebook."

"Wow," I said.

That was all I could say.

I mean, my sister had become a humanoid underground dweller. There wasn't much romance in that. Or maybe there was. Maybe my sister read romances all day. Maybe she was trapped in those romances.

"I really thought she was going to be a writer," Mr. P said. "She kept writing in her book. And she kept working up the courage to show it to somebody. And then she just stopped."

"Why?" I asked.

"I don't know."

"You don't have any idea?"

"No, not really."

Had she been hanging on to her dream of being a writer, but only barely hanging on, and something made her let go?

That had to be it, right? Something bad had happened to her, right? I mean, she lived in the fricking basement. People just don't live and hide in basements if they're happy.

Of course, my sister isn't much different from my dad in that regard.

Whenever my father isn't off on a drinking binge, he spends most of his time in his bedroom, alone, watching TV.

He mostly watches basketball.

He never minds if I go in there and watch games with him.

But we never talk much. We just sit there quietly and watch the games. My dad doesn't even cheer for his favorite teams or players. He doesn't react much to the games at all.

I suppose he is depressed.

I suppose my sister is depressed.

I suppose the whole family is depressed.

But I still want to know exactly why my sister gave up on her dream of writing romance novels.

I mean, yeah, it is kind of a silly dream. What kind of Indian writes romance novels? But it is still pretty cool. I love the thought of reading my sister's books. I love the thought of walking into a bookstore and seeing her name on the cover of a big and beautiful novel.

Spokane River Heat by Mary Runs Away.

That would be very cool.

"She could still write a book," I said. "There's always time to change your life."

I almost gagged when I said that. I didn't even believe that. There's never enough time to change your life. You don't get to change your life, period. Shit, maybe I was trying to write a romance novel.

"Mary was a bright and shining star," Mr. P said. "And then she faded year by year until you could barely see her anymore."

Wow, Mr. P was a poet.

"And you're a bright and shining star, too," he said. "You're the smartest kid in the school. And I don't want you to fail. I don't want you to fade away. You deserve better."

I didn't feel smart.

"I want you to say it," Mr. P said.

"Say what?"

"I want you to say that you deserve better."

I couldn't say it. It wasn't true. I mean, I wanted to have it better, but I didn't deserve it. I was the kid who threw books at teachers.

"You are a good kid. You deserve the world."

Wow, I wanted to cry. No teacher had ever said anything so nice, so incredibly nice, to me.

"Thank you," I said.

"You're welcome," he said. "Now say it."

"I can't."

And then I did cry. Tears rolled down my cheeks. I felt so weak.

"I'm sorry," I said.

"You don't have to be sorry for anything," he said. "Well, you better be sorry for hitting me, but you don't have to feel bad about crying."

"I don't like to cry," I said. "Other kids, they beat me up when I cry. Sometimes they make me cry so they can beat me up for crying."

"I know," he said. "And we let it happen. We let them pick on you."

"Rowdy protects me."

"I know Rowdy is your best friend, but he's, he's, he's, he's —," Mr. P stuttered. He wasn't sure what to say or do. "You know that Rowdy's dad hits him, don't you?"

"Yeah," I said. Whenever he came to school with a black eye, Rowdy made sure to give black eyes to two kids picked at random.

"Rowdy is just going to get meaner and meaner," Mr. P said.

"I know Rowdy has a temper and stuff, and he doesn't get good grades or anything, but he's been nice to me since we were kids. Since we were babies. I don't even know why he's been nice."

"I know, I know," Mr. P said. "But, listen, I want to tell

you something else. And you have to promise me you'll never repeat it."

"Okay," I said.

"Promise me."

"Okay, okay, I promise I won't repeat it."

"Not to anyone. Not even your parents."

"Nobody."

"Okay, then," he said and leaned closer to me because he didn't even want the trees to hear what he was going to say. "You have to leave this reservation."

"I'm going to Spokane with my dad later."

"No, I mean you have to leave the rez *forever.*"

"What do you mean?"

"You were right to throw that book at me. I deserved to get smashed in the face for what I've done to Indians. Every white person on this rez should get smashed in the face. But, let me tell you this. All the Indians should get smashed in the face, too."

I was shocked. Mr. P was *furious.*

"The only thing you kids are being taught is how to give up. Your friend Rowdy, he's given up. That's why he likes to hurt people. He wants them to feel as bad as he does."

"He doesn't hurt me."

"He doesn't hurt you because you're the only good thing in his life. He doesn't want to give that up. It's the only thing he hasn't given up."

Mr. P grabbed me by the shoulders and leaned so close to me that I could smell his breath.

Onions and garlic and hamburger and shame and pain.

"All these kids have given up," he said. "All your friends. All the bullies. And their mothers and fathers have given up, too. And their grandparents gave up and their grandparents before them. And me and every other teacher here. We're all defeated."

Mr. P was crying.

I couldn't believe it.

I'd never seen a sober adult cry.

"But not you," Mr. P said. "You can't give up. You won't give up. You threw that book in my face because somewhere inside you refuse to give up."

I didn't know what he was talking about. Or maybe I just didn't want to know.

Jeez, it was a lot of pressure to put on a kid. I was carrying the burden of my race, you know? I was going to get a bad back from it.

"If you stay on this rez," Mr. P said, "they're going to kill you. I'm going to kill you. We're all going to kill you. You can't fight us forever."

"I don't want to fight anybody," I said.

"You've been fighting since you were born," he said. "You fought off that brain surgery. You fought off those seizures. You fought off all the drunks and drug addicts. You kept your hope. And now, you have to take your hope and go somewhere where other people have hope."

I was starting to understand. He was a math teacher. I had to add my hope to somebody else's hope. I had to multiply hope by hope.

"Where is hope?" I asked. "Who has hope?"

"Son," Mr. P said. "You're going to find more and more hope the farther and farther you walk away from this sad, sad, sad reservation."

Go Means Go

After Mr. P left, I sat on the porch for a long time and thought about my life. What the heck was I supposed to do? I felt like life had just knocked me on my ass.

I was so happy when Mom and Dad got home from work.

"Hey, little man," Dad said.

"Hey, Dad, Mom."

"Junior, why are you looking so sad?" Mom asked. She knew stuff.

I didn't know how to start, so I just started with the biggest question.

all ass-kicking
bruises look
like **Texas**... →

"Who has the most hope?" I asked.

Mom and Dad looked at each other. They studied each other's eyes, you know, like they had antennas and were sending radio signals to each other. And then they both looked back at me.

"Come on," I said. "Who has the most hope?"

"White people," my parents said at the same time.

That's exactly what I thought they were going to say, so I said the most surprising thing they'd ever heard from me.

"I want to transfer schools," I said.

"You want to go to Hunters?" Mom said.

It's another school on the west end of the reservation, filled with poor Indians and poorer white kids. Yes, there is a place in the world where the white people are poorer than the Indians.

"No," I said.

"You want to go to Springdale?" Dad asked.

It's a school on the reservation border filled with the poorest Indians and poorer-than-poorest white kids. Yes, there is a place in the world where the white people are even poorer than you ever thought possible.

"I want to go to Reardan," I said.

Reardan is the rich, white farm town that sits in the wheat fields exactly twenty-two miles away from the rez. And it's a hick town, I suppose, filled with farmers and rednecks and racist cops who stop every Indian that drives through.

During one week when I was little, Dad got stopped three times for DWI: Driving While Indian.

But Reardan has one of the best small schools in the state, with a computer room and huge chemistry lab and a drama club and two basketball gyms.

The kids in Reardan are the smartest and most athletic kids anywhere. They are the best.

"I want to go to Reardan," I said again. I couldn't believe I was saying it. For me, it seemed as real as saying, "I want to fly to the moon."

"Are you sure?" my parents asked.

"Yes," I said.

"When do you want to go?" my parents asked.

"Right now," I said. "Tomorrow."

"Are you sure?" my parents asked. "You could maybe wait until the semester break. Or until next year. Get a fresh start."

"No, if I don't go now, I never will. I have to do it now."

"Okay," they said.

Yep, it was that easy with my parents. It was almost like they'd been waiting for me to ask them if I could go to Reardan, like they were psychics or something.

I mean, they've always known that I'm weird and ambitious, so maybe they expect me to do the weirdest things possible. And going to Reardan is truly a strange idea. But it isn't weird that my parents so quickly agreed with my plans. They want a better life for my sister and me. My sister is running away to get lost, but I am running away because I want to find *something*. And my parents love me so much that they want to help me. Yeah, Dad is a drunk and Mom is an ex-drunk, but they don't want their kids to be drunks.

"It's going to be hard to get you to Reardan," Dad said. "We can't afford to move there. And there ain't no school bus going to come out here."

"You'll be the first one to ever leave the rez this way," Mom said. "The Indians around here are going to be angry with you."

Shoot, I figure that my fellow tribal members are going to torture me.

Rowdy Sings the Blues

✳

So the day after I decided to transfer to Reardan, and after my parents agreed to make it happen, I walked over to the tribal school, and found Rowdy sitting in his usual place on the playground.

He was alone, of course. Everybody was scared of him.

"I thought you were on suspension, dickwad," he said, which was Rowdy's way of saying, "I'm happy you're here."

"Kiss my ass," I said.

I wanted to tell him that he was my best friend and I loved

him like crazy, but boys didn't say such things to other boys, and *nobody* said such things to Rowdy.

"Can I tell you a secret?" I asked.

"It better not be girly," he said.

"It's not."

"Okay, then, tell me."

"I'm transferring to Reardan."

Rowdy's eyes narrowed. His eyes always narrowed right before he beat the crap out of someone. I started shaking.

"That's not funny," he said.

"It's not supposed to be funny," I said. "I'm transferring to Reardan. I want you to come with me."

"And when are you going on this imaginary journey?"

"It's not imaginary. It's real. And I'm transferring now. I start school tomorrow at Reardan."

"You better quit saying that," he said. "You're getting me mad."

I didn't want to get him mad. When Rowdy got mad it took him days to get un-mad. But he was my best friend and I wanted him to know the truth.

"I'm not trying to get you mad," I said. "I'm telling the truth. I'm leaving the rez, man, and I want you to come with me. Come on. It will be an adventure."

"I don't even drive through that town," he said. "What makes you think I want to go to school there?"

He got up, stared me hard in the eyes, and then spit on the floor.

Last year, during eighth grade, we traveled to Reardan to play them in flag football. Rowdy was our star quarterback and kicker and middle linebacker, and I was the loser water boy, and we lost to Reardan by the score of 45–0.

Of course, losing isn't exactly fun.

Nobody wants to be a loser.

We all got really mad and vowed to kick their asses the next game.

But, two weeks after that, Reardan came to the rez and beat us 56–10.

During basketball season, Reardan beat us 72–45 and 86–50, our only two losses of the season.

Rowdy scored twenty-four points in the first game and forty in the second game.

I scored nine points in each game, going 3 for 10 on three-pointers in the first game and 3 for 15 in the second. Those were my two worst games of the season.

During baseball season, Rowdy hit three home runs in the first game against Reardan and two home runs in the second but we still lost by scores of 17–3 and 12–2. I played in both losses and struck out seven times and was hit by a pitch once.

Sad thing is, getting hit like that was my only hit of the season.

After baseball season, I led the Wellpinit Junior High Academic Bowl team against Reardan Junior High, and we lost by a grand total of 50–1.

Yep, we answered one question correctly.

I was the only kid, white or Indian, who knew that Charles Dickens wrote *A Tale of Two Cities*. And let me tell you, we Indians were the worst of times and those Reardan kids were the best of times.

Those kids were *magnificent*.

They knew *everything*.

And they were *beautiful*.

They were beautiful and smart.

They were beautiful and smart and epic.

They were filled with hope.

I don't know if hope is white. But I do know that hope for me is like some mythical creature:

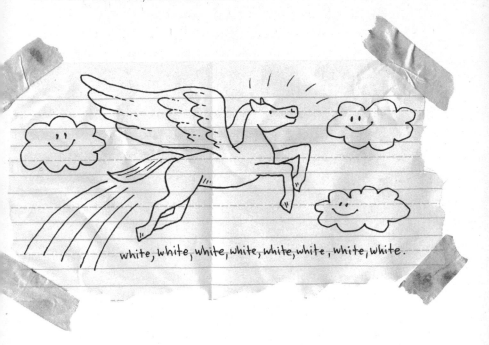

white, white, white, white, white, white, white, white.

Man, I was scared of those Reardan kids, and maybe I was scared of hope, too, but Rowdy absolutely hated all of it.

"Rowdy," I said. "I am going to Reardan tomorrow."

For the first time he saw that I was serious, but he didn't want me to be serious.

"You'll never do it," he said. "You're too scared."

"I'm going," I said.

"No way, you're a wuss."

"I'm doing it."

"You're a pussy."

"I'm going to Reardan tomorrow."

"You're really serious?"

"Rowdy," I said. "I'm as serious as a tumor."

He coughed and turned away from me. I touched his shoulder. Why did I touch his shoulder? I don't know. I was stupid. Rowdy spun around and shoved me.

"Don't touch me, you retarded fag!" he yelled.

My heart broke into fourteen pieces, one for each year that Rowdy and I had been best friends.

I started crying.

That wasn't surprising at all, but Rowdy started crying, too, and he hated that. He wiped his eyes, stared at his wet hand, and screamed. I'm sure that everybody on the rez heard that scream. It was the worst thing I'd ever heard.

It was pain, pure pain.

"Rowdy, I'm sorry," I said. "I'm sorry."

He kept screaming.

"You can still come with me," I said. "You're still my best friend."

Rowdy stopped screaming with his mouth but he kept screaming with his eyes.

"You always thought you were better than me," he yelled.

"No, no, I don't think I'm better than anybody. I think I'm worse than everybody else."

"Why are you leaving?"

"I have to go. I'm going to die if I don't leave."

I touched his shoulder again and Rowdy flinched.

Yes, I touched him again.

What kind of idiot was I?

I was the kind of idiot that got punched hard in the face by his best friend.

Bang! Rowdy punched me.

Bang! I hit the ground.

Bang! My nose bled like a firework.

I stayed on the ground for a long time after Rowdy walked away. I stupidly hoped that time would stand still if I stayed still. But I had to stand eventually, and when I did, I knew that my best friend had become my worst enemy.

How to Fight Monsters

*

The next morning, Dad drove me the twenty-two miles to Reardan.

"I'm scared," I said.

"I'm scared, too," Dad said.

He hugged me close. His breath smelled like mouthwash and lime vodka.

"You don't have to do this," he said. "You can always go back to the rez school."

"No," I said. "I have to do this."

Can you imagine what would have happened to me if I'd turned around and gone back to the rez school?

I would have been pummeled. Mutilated. Crucified.

You can't just betray your tribe and then change your mind ten minutes later. I was on a one-way bridge. There was no way to turn around, even if I wanted to.

"Just remember this," my father said. "Those white people aren't better than you."

But he was so wrong. And he knew he was wrong. He was the loser Indian father of a loser Indian son living in a world built for winners.

But he loved me so much. He hugged me even closer.

"This is a great thing," he said. "You're so brave. You're a warrior."

It was the best thing he could have said.

"Hey, here's some lunch money," he said and handed me a dollar.

We were poor enough to get free lunch, but I didn't want to be the only Indian *and* a sad sack who needed charity.

"Thanks, Dad," I said.

"I love you," he said.

"I love you, too."

I felt stronger so I stepped out of the car and walked to the front door. It was locked.

So I stood alone on the sidewalk and watched my father drive away. I hoped he'd drive right home and not stop in a bar and spend whatever money he had left.

I hoped he'd remember to come back and pick me up after school.

I stood alone at the front door for a few very long minutes.

It was still early and I had a black eye from Rowdy's good-bye punch. No, I had a purple, blue, yellow, and black eye. It looked like modern art.

Then the white kids began arriving for school. They surrounded me. Those kids weren't just white. They were *translucent*. I could see the blue veins running through their skin like rivers.

Most of the kids were my size or smaller, but there were ten or twelve monster dudes. Giant white guys. They looked like men, not boys. They had to be seniors. Some of them looked like they had to shave two or three times a day.

They stared at me, the Indian boy with the black eye and swollen nose, my going-away gifts from Rowdy. Those white kids couldn't believe their eyes. They stared at me like I was Bigfoot or a UFO. What was I doing at Reardan, whose mascot was an Indian, thereby making me the only *other* Indian in town?

bright red →

← REARDAN'S INSPIRING MASCOT.

So what was I doing in racist Reardan, where more than half of every graduating class went to college? Nobody in my family had ever gone near a college.

Reardan was the opposite of the rez. It was the opposite of my family. It was the opposite of me. I didn't deserve to be there. I knew it; all of those kids knew it. Indians don't deserve shit.

So, feeling worthless and stupid, I just waited. And pretty soon, a janitor opened the front door and all of the other kids strolled inside.

I stayed outside.

Maybe I could just drop out of school completely. I could go live in the woods like a hermit.

Like a real Indian.

Of course, since I was allergic to pretty much every plant that grew on earth, I would have been a real Indian with a head full of snot.

"Okay," I said to myself. "Here I go."

I walked into the school, made my way to the front office, and told them who I was.

"Oh, you're the one from the reservation," the secretary said.

"Yeah," I said.

I couldn't tell if she thought the reservation was a good or bad thing.

"My name is Melinda," she said. "Welcome to Reardan High School. Here's your schedule, a copy of the school constitution and moral code, and a temporary student ID. We've got you assigned to Mr. Grant for homeroom. You better hustle on down there. You're late."

"Ah, where is that?" I asked.

"We've only got one hallway here," she said and smiled. She had red hair and green eyes and was kind of sexy for an old woman. "It's all the way down on the left."

I shoved the paperwork into my backpack and hustled down to my homeroom.

I paused a second at the door and then walked inside.

Everybody, all of the students and the teacher, stopped to stare at me.

They stared hard.

Like I was bad weather.

"Take your seat," the teacher said. He was a muscular guy. He had to be a football coach.

I walked down the aisle and sat in the back row and tried to ignore all the stares and whispers, until a blond girl leaned over toward me.

Penelope!

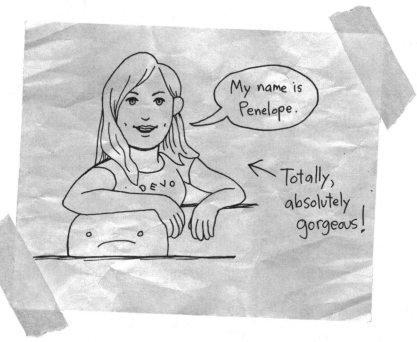

Yes, there are places left in the world where people are named Penelope!

I was emotionally erect.

"What's your name?" Penelope asked.

"Junior," I said.

She laughed and told her girlfriend at the next desk that

my name was Junior. They both laughed. Word spread around the room and pretty soon everybody was laughing.

They were laughing at *my name*.

I had no idea that Junior was a weird name. It's a common name on my rez, on any rez. You walk into any trading post on any rez in the United States and shout, "Hey, Junior!" and seventeen guys will turn around.

And three women.

But there were no other people named Junior in Reardan, so I was being laughed at because I was the only one who had that silly name.

And then I felt smaller because the teacher was taking roll and he called out my *name* name.

"Arnold Spirit," the teacher said.

No, he yelled it.

He was so big and muscular that his whisper was probably a scream.

"Here," I said as quietly as possible. My whisper was only a whisper.

"Speak up," the teacher said.

"Here," I said.

"My name is Mr. Grant," he said.

"I'm here, Mr. Grant."

He moved on to other students, but Penelope leaned over toward me again, but she wasn't laughing at all. She was mad now.

"I thought you said your name was Junior," Penelope said.

She *accused* me of telling her my *real* name. Well, okay, it wasn't completely my real name. My full name is Arnold Spirit Jr. But nobody calls me that. Everybody calls me Junior. Well, every other *Indian* calls me Junior.

"My name is Junior," I said. "And my name is Arnold. It's Junior and Arnold. I'm both."

I felt like two different people inside of one body.

No, I felt like a magician slicing myself in half, with Junior living on the north side of the Spokane River and Arnold living on the south.

"Where are you from?" she asked.

She was so pretty and her eyes were so blue.

I was suddenly aware that she was the prettiest girl I had ever seen up close. She was movie star pretty.

"Hey," she said. "I asked you where you're from."

Wow, she was tough.

"Wellpinit," I said. "Up on the rez, I mean, the reservation."

"Oh," she said. "That's why you talk so funny."

And yes, I had that stutter and lisp, but I also had that singsong reservation accent that made everything I said sound like a bad poem.

Man, I was freaked.

I didn't say another word for six days.

And on the seventh day, I got into the weirdest fistfight of my life. But before I tell you about the weirdest fistfight of my life, I have to tell you:

THE UNOFFICIAL AND UNWRITTEN
(but you better follow them or you're going to get beaten twice as hard)
SPOKANE INDIAN RULES OF FISTICUFFS:

1. IF SOMEBODY INSULTS YOU, THEN YOU HAVE TO FIGHT HIM.
2. IF YOU THINK SOMEBODY IS GOING TO INSULT YOU, THEN YOU HAVE TO FIGHT HIM.
3. IF YOU THINK SOMEBODY IS THINKING ABOUT INSULTING YOU, THEN YOU HAVE TO FIGHT HIM.
4. IF SOMEBODY INSULTS ANY OF YOUR FAMILY OR FRIENDS, OR IF YOU THINK THEY'RE GOING TO INSULT

YOUR FAMILY OR FRIENDS, OR IF YOU THINK THEY'RE
THINKING ABOUT INSULTING YOUR FAMILY OR FRIENDS,
THEN YOU HAVE TO FIGHT HIM.

5. YOU SHOULD NEVER FIGHT A GIRL, UNLESS SHE INSULTS
   YOU, YOUR FAMILY, OR YOUR FRIENDS, THEN YOU HAVE TO
   FIGHT HER.

6. IF SOMEBODY BEATS UP YOUR FATHER OR YOUR MOTHER,
   THEN YOU HAVE TO FIGHT THE SON AND/OR DAUGHTER
   OF THE PERSON WHO BEAT UP YOUR MOTHER OR FATHER.

7. IF YOUR MOTHER OR FATHER BEATS UP SOMEBODY, THEN
   THAT PERSON'S SON AND/OR DAUGHTER WILL FIGHT YOU.

8. YOU MUST ALWAYS PICK FIGHTS WITH THE SONS AND/OR
   DAUGHTERS OF ANY INDIANS WHO WORK FOR THE BUREAU
   OF INDIAN AFFAIRS.

9. YOU MUST ALWAYS PICK FIGHTS WITH THE SONS AND/OR
   DAUGHTERS OF ANY WHITE PEOPLE WHO LIVE ANY-
   WHERE ON THE RESERVATION.

10. IF YOU GET IN A FIGHT WITH SOMEBODY WHO IS SURE
    TO BEAT YOU UP, THEN YOU MUST THROW THE FIRST
    PUNCH, BECAUSE IT'S THE ONLY PUNCH YOU'LL EVER
    GET TO THROW.

11. IN ANY FIGHT, THE LOSER IS THE FIRST ONE WHO CRIES.

I knew those rules. I'd memorized those rules. I'd lived my
life by those rules. I got into my first fistfight when I was three
years old, and I'd been in dozens since.

My all-time record was five wins and one hundred and
twelve losses.

Yes, I was a terrible fighter.

I was a human punching bag.

I lost fights to boys, girls, and kids half my age.

One bully, Micah, made me beat up myself. Yes, he made
me punch myself in the face three times. I am the only

Indian in the history of the world who ever lost a fight *with himself.*

Okay, so now that you know about the rules, then I can tell you that I went from being a small target in Wellpinit to being a larger target in Reardan.

Well, let's get something straight. All of those pretty, pretty, pretty, pretty white girls ignored me. But that was okay. Indian girls ignored me, too, so I was used to it.

And let's face it, most of the white boys ignored me, too. But there were a few of those Reardan boys, the big jocks, who paid special attention to me. None of those guys punched me or got violent. After all, I was a reservation Indian, and no matter how geeky and weak I appeared to be, I was still a potential killer. So mostly they called me names. Lots of names.

And yeah, those were bad enough names. But I could handle them, especially when some huge monster boy was insulting me. But I knew I'd have to put a stop to it eventually or I'd always be known as "Chief" or "Tonto" or "Squaw Boy."

But I was scared.

I wasn't scared of fistfighting with those boys. I'd been in plenty of fights. And I wasn't scared of losing fights with them, either. I'd lost most every fight I'd been in. I was afraid those monsters were going to kill me.

And I don't mean "kill" as in "metaphor." I mean "kill" as in "beat me to death."

So, weak and poor and scared, I let them call me names while I tried to figure out what to do. And it might have continued that way if Roger the Giant hadn't taken it too far.

It was lunchtime and I was standing outside by the weird sculpture that was supposed to be an Indian. I was studying the sky like I was an astronomer, except it was daytime and I didn't have a telescope, so I was just an idiot.

Roger the Giant and his gang of giants strutted over to me.

"Hey, Chief," Roger said.

It seemed like he was seven feet tall and three hundred pounds. He was a farm boy who carried squealing pigs around like they were already thin slices of bacon.

I stared at Roger and tried to look tough. I read once that you can scare away a charging bear if you wave your arms and look big. But I figured I'd just look like a terrified idiot having an arm seizure.

"Hey, Chief," Roger said. "You want to hear a joke?"

"Sure," I said.

"Did you know that Indians are living proof that niggers fuck buffalo?"

I felt like Roger had kicked me in the face. That was the most racist thing I'd ever heard in my life.

Roger and his friends were laughing like crazy. I hated them. And I knew I had to do something big. I couldn't let them get away with that shit. I wasn't just defending myself. I was defending Indians, black people, *and* buffalo.

So I punched Roger in the face.

He wasn't laughing when he landed on his ass. And he wasn't laughing when his nose bled like red fireworks.

I struck some fake karate pose because I figured Roger's gang was going to attack me for bloodying their leader.

But they just stared at me.

They were *shocked.*

"You punched me," Roger said. His voice was thick with blood. "I can't believe you punched me."

He sounded insulted.

He sounded like his *poor little feelings* had been hurt.

I couldn't believe it.

He acted like he was the one who'd been wronged.

"You're an animal," he said.

I felt brave all of a sudden. Yeah, maybe it was just a stupid and immature school yard fight. Or maybe it was the most important moment of my life. Maybe I was telling the world that I was no longer a human target.

"You meet me after school right here," I said.

"Why?" he asked.

I couldn't believe he was so stupid.

"Because we're going to finish this fight."

"You're crazy," Roger said.

He got to his feet and walked away. His gang stared at me like I was a serial killer, and then they followed their leader.

I was absolutely confused.

I had followed the rules of fighting. I had behaved exactly the way I was supposed to behave. But these white boys had ignored the rules. In fact, they followed a whole other set of mysterious rules where people apparently DID NOT GET INTO FISTFIGHTS.

"Wait," I called after Roger.

"What do you want?" Roger asked.

"What are the rules?"

"What rules?"

I didn't know what to say, so I just stood there red and mute like a stop sign. Roger and his friends disappeared.

I felt like somebody had shoved me into a rocket ship and blasted me to a new planet. I was a freaky alien and there was absolutely no way to get home.

Grandmother Gives Me Some Advice

*

I went home that night completely confused. And terrified.

If I'd punched an Indian in the face, then he would have spent days plotting his revenge. And I imagined that white guys would also want revenge after getting punched in the face. So I figured Roger was going to run me over with a farm tractor or combine or grain truck or runaway pig.

I wished Rowdy was still my friend. I could have sent him after Roger. It would have been like King Kong battling Godzilla.

I realized how much of my self-worth, my sense of safety, was based on Rowdy's fists.

But Rowdy hated me. And Roger hated me.

I was good at being hated by guys who could kick my ass. It's not a talent you really want to have.

My mother and father weren't home, so I turned to my grandmother for advice.

"Grandma," I said. "I punched this big guy in the face. And he just walked away. And now I'm afraid he's going to kill me."

"Why did you punch him?" she asked.

"He was bullying me."

"You should have just walked away."

"He called me 'chief.' And 'squaw boy.'"

"Then you should have kicked him in the balls."

She pretended to kick a big guy in the crotch and we both laughed.

"Did he hit you?" she asked.

"No, not at all," I said.

"Not even after you hit him?"

"Nope."

"And he's a big guy?"

"Gigantic. I bet he could take Rowdy down."

"Wow," she said.

"It's strange, isn't it?" I asked. "What does it mean?"

Grandma thought hard for a while.

"I think it means he respects you," she said.

"Respect? No way!"

"Yes way! You see, you men and boys are like packs of wild dogs. This giant boy is the alpha male of the school, and you're the new dog, so he pushed you around a bit to see how tough you are."

"But I'm not tough at all," I said.

MY GRANDMOTHER

Her best dish is SALMON MUSH

(much better than it sounds)

bandanna on her head, always (red when she goes to powwows, green around the house, blue when she visits her friends, purple when she goes to garage sales)

belt used to belong to my grandfather, who died when I was a baby

house dress purchased in 1972 for $10

RODEO KING

makes her living selling beaded keychains on eBay ("Highly Sacred Aboriginal Transportation Charms")

basketball sneakers because "she's got mad skills."

"Yeah, but you punched the alpha dog in the face," she said. "They're going to respect you now."

"I love you, Grandma," I said. "But you're crazy."

I couldn't sleep that night because I kept thinking about my impending doom. I knew Roger would be waiting for me in the morning at school. I knew he'd punch me in the head and shoulder area about two hundred times. I knew I'd soon be in a hospital drinking soup through a straw.

So, exhausted and terrified, I went to school.

My day began as it usually did. I got out of bed at dark-thirty, and rummaged around the kitchen for anything to eat. All I could find was a package of orange fruit drink mix, so I made a gallon of that, and drank it all down.

Then I went into the bedroom and asked Mom and Dad if they were driving me to school.

"Don't have enough gas," Dad said and went back to sleep.

Great, I'd have to walk.

So I put on my shoes and coat, and started down the highway. I got lucky because my dad's best friend Eugene just happened to be heading to Spokane.

Eugene was a good guy, and like an uncle to me, but he was drunk all the time. Not stinky drunk, just drunk enough to be drunk. He was a funny and kind drunk, always wanting to laugh and hug you and sing songs and dance.

Funny how the saddest guys can be happy drunks.

"Hey, Junior," he said. "Hop on my pony, man."

So I hopped onto the back of Eugene's bike, and off we went, barely in control. I just closed my eyes and held on.

And pretty soon, Eugene got me to school.

We pulled up in front and a lot of my classmates just stared. I mean, Eugene had braids down to his butt, for one, and neither of us wore helmets, for the other.

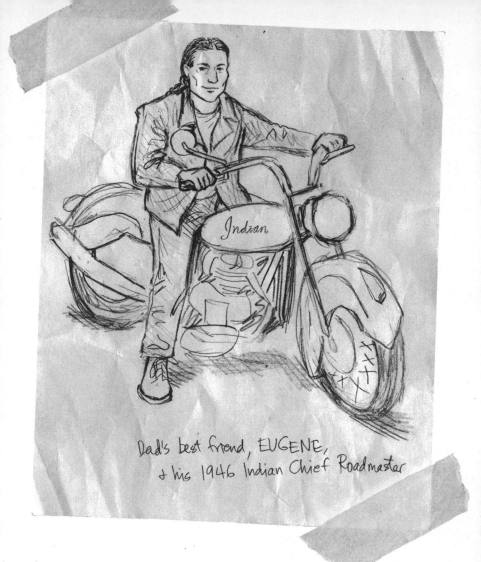

Dad's best friend, EUGENE,
+ his 1946 Indian Chief Roadmaster

I suppose we looked *dangerous*.

"Man," he said. "There's a lot of white people here."

"Yeah."

"You doing all right with them?"

"I don't know. I guess."

"It's pretty cool, you doing this," he said.

"You think?"

"Yeah, man, I could never do it. I'm a wuss."

Wow, I felt proud.

"Thanks for the ride," I said.

"You bet," Eugene said.

He laughed and buzzed away. I walked up to the school and tried to ignore the stares of my classmates.

And then I saw Roger walk out the front door.

Man, I was going to have to fight. Shit, my whole life is a fight.

"Hey," Roger said.

"Hey," I said.

"Who was that on the bike?" he asked.

"Oh, that was my dad's best friend."

"That was a cool bike," he said. "Vintage."

"Yeah, he just got it."

"You ride with him a lot?"

"Yes," I said. I lied.

"Cool," Roger said.

"Yeah, cool," I said.

"All right, then," he said. "I'll see you around."

And then he walked away.

Wow, he didn't kick my ass. He was actually nice. He paid me some respect. He paid respect to Eugene and his bike.

Maybe Grandma was right. Maybe I had challenged the alpha dog and was now being rewarded for it.

I love my grandmother. She's the smartest person on the planet.

Feeling almost like a human being, I walked into the school and saw Penelope the Beautiful.

"Hey, Penelope," I said, hoping that she knew I was now accepted by the dog pack.

She didn't even respond to me. Maybe she hadn't heard me.

"Hey, Penelope," I said again.

She looked at me and sniffed.

SHE SNIFFED!

LIKE I SMELLED BAD OR SOMETHING!

"Do I know you?" she said.

There were only about one hundred students in the whole school, right? So of course, she knew me. She was just being a bitch.

"I'm Junior," I said. "I mean, I'm Arnold."

"Oh, that's right," she said. "You're the boy who can't figure out his own name."

Her friends giggled.

I was so ashamed. I might have impressed the king, but the queen still hated me. I guess my grandmother didn't know everything.

Tears of a Clown
✵

When I was twelve, I fell in love with an Indian girl named Dawn. She was tall and brown and was the best traditional powwow dancer on the rez. Her braids, wrapped in otter fur, were legendary. Of course, she didn't care about me. She mostly made fun of me (she called me Junior High Honky for some reason I never understood). But that just made me love her even more. She was out of my league, and even though I was only twelve, I knew that I'd be one of those guys who always fell in love with the unreachable, ungettable, and uninterested.

One night, at about two in the morning, when Rowdy slept over at my house, I made a full confession.

"Man," I said. "I love Dawn so much."

He was pretending to be asleep on the floor of my room.

"Rowdy," I said. "Are you awake?"

"No."

"Did you hear what I said?"

"No."

"I said I love Dawn so much."

He was quiet.

"Aren't you going to say anything?" I asked.

"About what?"

"About what I just said."

"I didn't hear you say anything."

He was just screwing with me.

"Come on, Rowdy, I'm trying to tell you something major."

"You're just being stupid," he said.

"What's so stupid about it?"

"Dawn doesn't give a shit about you," he said.

And that made me cry. Man, I've always cried too easily. I cry when I'm happy or sad. I cry when I'm angry. I cry because I'm crying. It's weak. It's the opposite of warrior.

"Quit crying," Rowdy said.

"I can't help it," I said. "I love her more than I've ever loved anybody."

Yeah, I was quite the dramatic twelve-year-old.

"Please," Rowdy said. "Stop that bawling, okay?"

"Okay, okay," I said. "I'm sorry."

I wiped my face with one of my pillows and threw it across the room.

"Jesus, you're a wimp," Rowdy said.

"Just don't tell anybody I cried about Dawn," I said.

"Have I ever told anybody your secrets?" Rowdy asked.

"No."

"Okay, then, I won't tell anybody you cried over a dumb girl."

And he didn't tell anybody. Rowdy was my secret-keeper.

Halloween

✳

At school today, I went dressed as a homeless dude. It was a pretty easy costume for me. There's not much difference between my good and bad clothes, so I pretty much look half-homeless anyway.

And Penelope went dressed as a homeless woman. Of course, she was the most beautiful homeless woman who ever lived.

We made a cute couple.

Of course, we weren't a couple at all, but I still found the need to comment on our common taste.

"Hey," I said. "We have the same costume."

I thought she was just going to sniff at me again, but she almost smiled.

"You have a good costume," Penelope said. "You look really homeless."

"Thank you," I said. "You look really cute."

"I'm not trying to be cute," she said. "I'm wearing this to protest the treatment of homeless people in this country. I'm going to ask for only spare change tonight, instead of candy, and I'm going to give it all to the homeless."

I didn't understand how wearing a Halloween costume could become a political statement, but I admired her commitment. I wanted her to admire my commitment, too. So I lied.

"Well," I said. "I'm wearing this to protest the treatment of homeless Native Americans in this country."

"Oh," she said. "I guess that's pretty cool."

"Yeah, that spare change thing is a good idea. I think I might do that, too."

Of course, after school, I'd be trick-or-treating on the rez, so I wouldn't collect as much spare change as Penelope would in Reardan.

"Hey," I said. "Why don't we pool our money tomorrow and send it together? We'd be able to give twice as much."

Penelope stared at me. She studied me. I think she was trying to figure out if I was serious.

"Are you for real?" she asked.

"Yes," I said.

"Well, okay," she said. "It's a deal."

"Cool, cool, cool," I said.

So, later that night, I went out trick-or-treating on the rez. It was a pretty stupid idea, I guess. I was probably too old to be trick-or-treating, even if I was asking for spare change for the homeless.

Oh, plenty of people were happy to give me spare change. And more than a few of them gave me candy *and* spare change.

And my dad was home and sober, and he gave me a dollar. He was almost always home and sober and generous on Halloween.

A few folks, especially the grandmothers, thought I was a brave little dude for going to a white school.

But there were a lot more people who just called me names and slammed the door in my face.

And I didn't even consider what other kids might do to me.

About ten o'clock, as I was walking home, three guys jumped me. I couldn't tell who they were. They all wore Frankenstein masks. And they shoved me to the ground and kicked me a few times.

And spit on me.

I could handle the kicks.

But the spit made me feel like an insect.

Like a slug.

Like a slug burning to death from salty spit.

They didn't beat me up too bad. I could tell they didn't want to put me in the hospital or anything. Mostly they just wanted to remind me that I was a traitor. And they wanted to steal my candy and the money.

It wasn't much. Maybe ten bucks in coins and dollar bills.

But that money, and the idea of giving it to poor people, had made me feel pretty good about myself.

I was a poor kid raising money for other poor people.

It made me feel almost honorable.

But I just felt stupid and naïve after those guys took off. I lay there in the dirt and remembered how Rowdy and I used to trick-or-treat together. We'd always wear the same costume. And I knew that if I'd been with him, I never would have gotten assaulted.

And then I wondered if Rowdy was one of the guys who just beat me up. Damn, that would be awful. But I couldn't believe it. I wouldn't believe it. No matter how much he hated me, Rowdy would never hurt me that way. Never.

At least, I hope he'd never hurt me.

The next morning, at school, I walked up to Penelope and showed her my empty hands.

"I'm sorry," I said.

"Sorry for what?" she asked.

"I raised money last night, but then some guys attacked me and stole it."

"Oh, my God, are you okay?"

"Yeah, they just kicked me a few times."

"Oh, my God, where did they kick you?"

I lifted up my shirt and showed her the bruises on my belly and ribs and back.

"That's terrible. Did you see a doctor?"

"Oh, they're not so bad," I said.

"That one looks like it really hurts," she said and touched a fingertip to the huge purple bruise on my back.

I almost fainted.

Her touch felt so good.

"I'm sorry they did that to you," she said. "I'll still put your name on the money when I send it."

"Wow," I said. "That's really cool. Thank you."

"You're welcome," she said and walked away.

I was just going to let her go. But I had to say something memorable, something huge.

"Hey!" I called after her.

"What?" she asked.

"It feels good, doesn't it?"

"What feels good?"

"It feels good to help people, doesn't it?" I asked.

"Yes," she said. "Yes, it does."

She smiled.

Of course, after that little moment, I thought that Penelope and I would become closer. I thought that she'd start paying more attention to me and that everybody else would notice and then I'd become the most popular dude in the place. But nothing much changed. I was still a stranger in a strange land. And Penelope still treated me pretty much the same. She didn't really say much to me. And I didn't really say much to her.

I wanted to ask Rowdy for his advice.

"Hey, buddy," I would have said. "How do I make a beautiful white girl fall in love with me?"

"Well, buddy," he would have said. "The first thing you have to do is change the way you look, the way you talk, and the way you walk. And then she'll think you're her fricking Prince Charming."

Slouching
Toward
Thanksgiving
✹

I walked like a zombie through the next few weeks in Reardan.

Well, no, that's not exactly the right description.

I mean, if I'd been walking around like a zombie, I might have been scary. So, no, I wasn't a zombie, not at all. Because you can't ignore a zombie. So that made me, well, it made me *nothing*.

Zero.

Zilch.

Nada.

In fact, if you think of everybody with a body, soul, and brain as a human, then I was the opposite of human.

It was the loneliest time of my life.

And whenever I get lonely, I grow a big zit on the end of my nose.

If things didn't get better soon, I was going to turn into one giant walking talking zit.

A strange thing was happening to me.

Zitty and lonely, I woke up on the reservation as an Indian, and somewhere on the road to Reardan, I became something less than Indian.

And once I arrived at Reardan, I became something less than less than less than Indian.

Those white kids did not talk to me.

They barely looked at me.

Well, Roger would nod his head at me, but he didn't socialize with me or anything. I wondered if maybe I should punch everybody in the face. Maybe they'd all pay attention to me then.

I just walked from class to class alone; I sat at lunch alone; during PE I stood in the corner of the gym and played catch with myself. Just tossed a basketball up and down, up and down, up and down.

And I know you're thinking, "Okay, Mr. Sad Sack, how many ways are you going to tell us how depressed you were?"

And, okay, maybe I'm overstating my case. Maybe I'm exaggerating. So let me tell you a few good things that I discovered during that awful time.

First of all, I learned that I was smarter than most of those white kids.

Oh, there were a couple girls and one boy who were little Einsteins, and there was no way I'd ever be smarter than them, but I was way smarter than 99 percent of the others. And not just smart for an Indian, okay? I was smart, period.

Let me give you an example.

In geology class, the teacher, Mr. Dodge, was talking about the petrified wood forests near George, Washington, on the Columbia River, and how it was pretty amazing that wood could turn into rock.

I raised my hand.

"Yes, Arnold," Mr. Dodge said.

He was surprised. That was the first time I'd raised my hand in his class.

"Uh, er, um," I said.

Yeah, I was so *articulate*.

"Spit it out," Dodge said.

"Well," I said. "Petrified wood is not wood."

My classmates stared at me. They couldn't believe that I was contradicting a teacher.

"If it's not wood," Dodge said, "then why do they call it wood?"

"I don't know," I said. "I didn't name the stuff. But I know how it works."

Dodge's face was red.

Hot red.

I'd never seen an Indian look that red. So why do they call us the redskins?

"Okay, Arnold, if you're so smart," Dodge said, "then tell us how it works."

"Well, what happens is, er, when you have wood that's buried under dirt, then minerals and stuff sort of, uh, soak into the wood. They, uh, kind of melt the wood and the glue that holds the wood together. And then the minerals sort of take the place of the wood and the glue. I mean, the minerals keep the same shape as the wood. Like, if the minerals took all the wood and glue out of a, uh, tree, then the tree would still be a tree, sort of, but it would be a tree made out of minerals. So, uh, you see, the wood has not turned into rocks. The rocks have replaced the wood."

Dodge stared hard at me. He was dangerously angry:

a volcano   Mr. Dodge

Which of these pyrotechnic giants will explode first?!?

"Okay, Arnold," Dodge said. "Where did you learn this fact? On the reservation? Yes, we all know there's so much amazing science on the reservation."

My classmates snickered. They pointed their fingers at me and giggled. Except for one. Gordy, the class genius. He raised his hand.

"Gordy," Dodge said, all happy and relieved and stuff. "I'm sure you can tell us the truth."

"Uh, actually," Gordy said, "Arnold is right about petrified wood. That's what happens."

Dodge suddenly went all pale. Yep. From blood red to snow white in about two seconds.

If Gordy said it was true, then it was true. And even Dodge knew that.

Mr. Dodge wasn't even a real science teacher. That's what happens in small schools, you know? Sometimes you don't have enough money to hire a real science teacher. Sometimes you have an old real science teacher who retires or quits and leaves you without a replacement. And if you don't have a real science teacher, then you pick one of the other teachers and make him the science teacher.

And that's why small-town kids sometimes don't know the truth about petrified wood.

"Well, isn't that interesting," the fake science teacher said. "Thank you for sharing that with us, Gordy."

Yeah, that's right.

Mr. Dodge thanked Gordy, but didn't say another word to me.

Yep, now even the teachers were treating me like an idiot.

I shrank back into my chair and remembered when I used to be a human being.

I remember when people used to think I was smart.

I remember when people used to think my brain was useful.

Damaged by water, sure. And ready to seizure at any moment. But still useful, and maybe even a little bit beautiful and sacred and magical.

After class, I caught up to Gordy in the hallway.

"Hey, Gordy," I said. "Thanks."

"Thanks for what?" he said.

"Thanks for sticking up for me back there. For telling Dodge the truth."

"I didn't do it for you," Gordy said. "I did it for science."

He walked away. I stood there and waited for the rocks to replace my bones and blood.

the brain of many colors

I rode the bus home that night.

Well, no, I rode the bus to the end of the line, which was the reservation border.

And there I waited.

My dad was supposed to pick me up. But he wasn't sure if he'd have enough gas money.

Especially if he was going to stop at the rez casino and play slot machines first.

I waited for thirty minutes.

Exactly.

Then I started walking.

Getting to school was always an adventure.

After school, I'd ride the bus to the end of the line and wait for my folks.

If they didn't come, I'd start walking.

Hitchhiking in the opposite direction.

Somebody was usually heading back home to the rez, so I'd usually catch a ride.

Three times, I had to walk the whole way home.

Twenty-two miles.

I got blisters each time.

Anyway, after my petrified wood day, I caught a ride with a Bureau of Indian Affairs white guy and he dropped me off right in front of my house.

I walked inside and saw that my mother was crying.

I often walked inside to find my mother crying.

"What's wrong?" I asked.

"It's your sister," she said.

"Did she run away again?"

"She got married."

Wow, I was freaked. But my mother and father were absolutely freaked. Indian families stick together like Gorilla Glue, the strongest adhesive in the world. My mother and father both lived within two miles of where they were born, and my grandmother lived one mile from where she was born. Ever since the Spokane Indian Reservation was founded back in 1881, nobody in my family had ever lived anywhere else. We Spirits stay in one place. We are absolutely tribal. For good or bad, we don't leave one another. And now, my mother and father had lost two kids to the outside world.

I think they felt like failures. Or maybe they were just lonely. Or maybe they didn't know what they were feeling.

I didn't know what to feel. Who could understand my sister?

After seven years of living in the basement and watching TV, after doing *absolutely nothing* at all, my sister decided she needed to change her life.

I guess I'd kind of shamed her.

If I was brave enough to go to Reardan, then she'd be brave enough to MARRY A FLATHEAD INDIAN AND MOVE TO MONTANA.

"Where'd she meet this guy?" I asked my mother.

"At the casino," she said. "Your sister said he was a good poker player. I guess he travels to all the Indian casinos in the country."

"She married him because he plays cards?"

"She said he wasn't afraid to gamble everything, and that's the kind of man she wanted to spend her life with."

I couldn't believe it. My sister married a guy for a damn silly reason. But I suppose people often get married for damn silly reasons.

"Is he good-looking?" I asked.

"He's actually kind of ugly," my mother said. "He has this hook nose and his eyes are way different sizes."

Damn, my sister had married a lopsided, eagle-nosed, nomadic poker player.

It made me feel smaller.

I thought I was pretty tough.

But I'd just have to dodge dirty looks from white kids while my sister would be dodging gunfire in beautiful Montana. Those Montana Indians were so tough that white people were scared of them.

Can you imagine a place where white people are scared of Indians and not the other way around?

That's Montana.

And my sister had married one of those crazy Indians.

She didn't even tell our parents or grandmother or me before she left. She called Mom from St. Ignatius, Montana, on the Flathead Indian Reservation, and said, "Hey, Mom, I'm a married woman now. I want to have ten babies and live here forever and ever."

How weird is that? It's almost *romantic*.

And then I realized that my sister was trying to LIVE a romance novel.

Man, that takes courage and imagination. Well, it also took some degree of mental illness, too, but I was suddenly happy for her.

And a little scared.

The Stranger from Montana

Think YOU'RE so tough, Junior?!

MY ONLY SISTER

AN EXCERPT FROM THE BOOK:

"I want to have ten babies and live here forever and ever!" exclaimed Mary Runs Away.

"Darling!" gushed what's-his-face. Their beer-smelly mouths met in a big kiss, until what's-his-face had to burp. "Bleeap!"

Well, a lot scared.

She was trying to live out her dream. We should have all been delirious that she'd moved out of the basement. We'd been trying to get her out of there for years. Of course, my mother and father would have been happy if she'd just gotten a part-time job at the post office or trading post, and maybe just moved into an upstairs bedroom in our house.

But I just kept thinking that my sister's spirit hadn't been killed. She hadn't given up. This reservation had tried to suffocate her, had kept her trapped in a basement, and now she was out roaming the huge grassy fields of Montana.

How cool!

I felt inspired.

Of course, my parents and grandmother were in shock. They thought my sister and I were going absolutely crazy.

But I thought we were being warriors, you know?

And a warrior isn't afraid of confrontation.

So I went to school the next day and walked right up to Gordy the Genius White Boy.

"Gordy," I said. "I need to talk to you."

"I don't have time," he said. "Mr. Orcutt and I have to debug some PCs. Don't you hate PCs? They are sickly and fragile and vulnerable to viruses. PCs are like French people living during the bubonic plague."

Wow, and people thought I was a freak.

"I much prefer Macs, don't you?" he asked. "They're so poetic."

This guy was in love with computers. I wondered if he was secretly writing a romance about a skinny, white boy genius who was having sex with a half-breed Apple computer.

"Computers are computers," I said. "One or the other, it's all the same."

Gordy sighed.

"So, Mr. Spirit," he said. "Are you going to bore me with your tautologies all day or are you going to actually say something?"

Tautologies? What the heck were tautologies? I couldn't ask Gordy because then he'd know I was an illiterate Indian idiot.

"You don't know what a tautology is, do you?" he asked.

"Yes, I do," I said. "Really, I do. Completely, I do."

"You're lying."

"No, I'm not."

"Yes, you are."

"How can you tell?"

"Because your eyes dilated, your breathing rate increased a little bit, and you started to sweat."

Okay, so Gordy was a human lie detector machine, too.

"All right, I lied," I said. "What is a tautology?"

Gordy sighed again.

I HATED THAT SIGH! I WANTED TO PUNCH THAT SIGH IN THE FACE!

"A tautology is a repetition of the same sense in different words," he said.

"Oh," I said.

What the hell was he talking about?

"It's a redundancy."

"Oh, you mean, redundant, like saying the same thing over and over but in different ways?"

"Yes."

"Oh, so if I said something like, 'Gordy is a dick without ears and an ear without a dick,' then that would be a tautology."

Gordy smiled.

"That's not exactly a tautology, but it is funny. You have a singular wit."

I laughed.

Gordy laughed, too. But then he realized that I wasn't laughing WITH him. I was laughing AT him.

"What's so funny?" he asked.

"I can't believe you said 'singular wit.' That's sounds like fricking British or something."

"Well, I am a bit of an Anglophile."

"An Anglophile? What's an Angophile?"

"It's someone who loves Mother England."

God, this kid was an eighty-year-old literature professor trapped in the body of a fifteen-year-old farm boy.

"Listen, Gordy," I said. "I know you're a genius and all. But you are one weird dude."

"I'm quite aware of my differences. I wouldn't classify them as weird."

"Don't get me wrong. I think weird is great. I mean, if you look at all the great people in history — Einstein, Michelangelo, Emily Dickinson — then you're looking at a bunch of weird people."

"I'm going to be late for class," Gordy said. "You're going to be late for class. Perhaps you should, as they say, cut to the chase."

I looked at Gordy. He was a big kid, actually, strong from bucking bales and driving trucks. He was probably the strongest geek in the world.

"I want to be your friend," I said.

"Excuse me?" he asked.

"I want us to be friends," I said.

Gordy stepped back.

"I assure you," he said. "I am not a homosexual."

"Oh, no," I said. "I don't want to be friends that way. I just meant regular friends. I mean, you and I, we have a lot in common."

Gordy studied me now.

I was an Indian kid from the reservation. I was lonely and sad and isolated and terrified.

Just like Gordy.

And so we did become friends. Not the best of friends. Not like Rowdy and me. We didn't share secrets. Or dreams.

No, we studied together.

Gordy taught me how to study.

Best of all, he taught me how to read.

"Listen," he said one afternoon in the library. "You have to read a book three times before you know it. The first time you read it for the story. The plot. The movement from scene to scene that gives the book its momentum, its rhythm. It's like riding a raft down a river. You're just paying attention to the currents. Do you understand that?"

"Not at all," I said.

"Yes, you do," he said.

"Okay, I do," I said. I really didn't, but Gordy believed in me. He wouldn't let me give up.

"The second time you read a book, you read it for its history. For its knowledge of history. You think about the meaning of each word, and where that word came from. I mean, you read a novel that has the word 'spam' in it, and you know where that word comes from, right?"

"Spam is junk e-mail," I said.

"Yes, that's what it is, but who invented the word, who first used it, and how has the meaning of the word changed since it was first used?"

"I don't know," I said.

"Well, you have to look all that up. If you don't treat each word that seriously then you're not treating the novel seriously."

I thought about my sister in Montana. Maybe romance novels were absolutely serious business. My sister certainly thought they were. I suddenly understood that if every moment of a book should be taken seriously, then every moment of a life should be taken seriously as well.

"I draw cartoons," I said.

"What's your point?" Gordy asked.

"I take them seriously. I use them to understand the world. I use them to make fun of the world. To make fun of people. And sometimes I draw people because they're my friends and family. And I want to honor them."

"So you take your cartoons as seriously as you take books?"

"Yeah, I do," I said. "That's kind of pathetic, isn't it?"

"No, not at all," Gordy said. "If you're good at it, and you love it, and it helps you navigate the river of the world, then it can't be wrong."

Wow, this dude was a poet. My cartoons weren't just good for giggles; they were also good for poetry. Funny poetry, but poetry nonetheless. It was seriously funny stuff.

"But don't take anything too seriously, either," Gordy said.

The little dork could read minds, too. He was like some kind of Star Wars alien creature with invisible tentacles that sucked your thoughts out of your brain.

"You read a book for the story, for each of its words," Gordy said, "and you draw your cartoons for the story, for each of the words and images. And, yeah, you need to take that seriously, but you should also read and draw because really good books and cartoons give you a boner."

I was shocked:

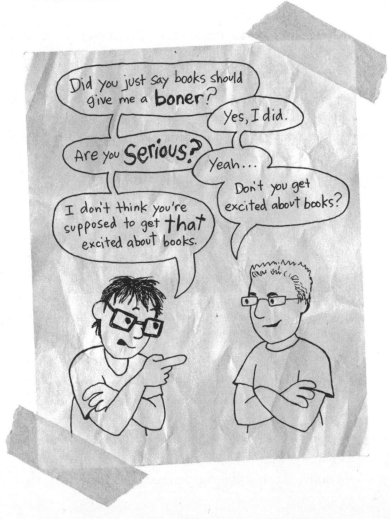

"You should get a boner! You have to get a boner!" Gordy shouted. "Come on!"

We ran into the Reardan High School Library.

"Look at all these books," he said.

"There aren't that many," I said. It was a small library in a small high school in a small town.

"There are three thousand four hundred and twelve books here," Gordy said. "I know that because I counted them."

"Okay, now you're officially a freak," I said.

"Yes, it's a small library. It's a tiny one. But if you read one of these books a day, it would still take you almost ten years to finish."

"What's your point?"

"The world, even the smallest parts of it, is filled with things you don't know."

Wow. That was a huge idea.

Any town, even one as small as Reardan, was a place of mystery. And that meant that Wellpinit, that smaller, Indian town, was also a place of mystery.

"Okay, so it's like each of these books is a mystery. Every book is a mystery. And if you read all the books ever written, it's like you've read one giant mystery. And no matter how much you learn, you just keep on learning there is so much more you need to learn."

"Yes, yes, yes, yes," Gordy said. "Now doesn't that give you a boner?"

"I am rock hard," I said.

Gordy blushed.

"Well, I don't mean boner in the sexual sense," Gordy said. "I don't think you should run through life with a real erect penis. But you should approach each book — you should approach life — with the real possibility that you might get a metaphorical boner at any point."

"A metaphorical boner!" I shouted. "What the heck is a metaphorical boner?"

Gordy laughed.

"When I say boner, I really mean joy," he said.

"Then why didn't you say joy? You didn't have to say boner. Whenever I think about boners, I get confused."

"Boner is funnier. And more joyful."

Gordy and I laughed.

He was an extremely weird dude. But he was the smartest person I'd ever known. He would always be the smartest person I'd ever known.

And he certainly helped me through school. He not only tutored me and challenged me, but he made me realize that hard work — that the act of finishing, of completing, of accomplishing a task — is joyous.

In Wellpinit, I was a freak because I loved books.

In Reardan, I was a joyous freak.

And my sister, she was a traveling freak.

We were the freakiest brother and sister in history.

My Sister Sends Me an E-mail ✳

From: Mary
Sent: Thursday, November 16, 2006 4:41 PM
To: Junior
Subject: Hi!

Dear Junior:

I love it here in Montana. It's beautiful. Yesterday, I rode a horse for the first time. Indians still ride horses in Montana. I'm still looking for a job. I've sent applications to all the restaurants on the reservation. Yep, the Flathead Rez has about twenty restaurants. It's weird. They have six or seven towns, too. Can you believe that? That's a lot of towns for one rez! And you know what's really weird? Some of the towns on the rez are filled with white people. I don't know how that happened. But the people who live in those white towns don't always like Indians much. One of those towns, called Polson, tried to secede (that means quit, I looked it up) from the rez. Really. It was like the Civil War. Even though the town is in the middle of the rez, the white folks in that town decided they didn't want to be a part of the rez. Crazy. But most of the people here are nice. The whites and Indians. And you know the best part? There's this really great hotel where hubby and I had our honeymoon. It's on Flathead Lake and we had a suite, a hotel room with its own separate bedroom! And there was a phone in the bathroom! Really! I could have called you from the bathoom. But that's not even the most crazy part. We decide to order room service, to have the food delivered to our room, and guess what they had on the menu? Indian fry bread! Yep. For five dollars, you could get fry bread. Crazy! So I ordered up two pieces. I didn't think it would be any good, especially not as good as grandma's. But let me tell you. It was great. Almost as good as grandma's. And they had the fry bread on this fancy plate and so I ate it with this fancy fork and knife. And I just kept imagining there was some Flathead Indian grandma in the kitchen, just making fry bread for all the room-service people. It was a dream come true! I love my life! I love my husband! I love Montana!

I love you!
Your sis, Mary

Thanksgiving

*

It was a snowless Thanksgiving.

We had a turkey, and Mom cooked it perfectly.

We also had mashed potatoes, gravy, green beans, corn, cranberry sauce, and pumpkin pie. It was a feast.

I always think it's funny when Indians celebrate Thanksgiving. I mean, sure, the Indians and Pilgrims were best friends during that first Thanksgiving, but a few years later, the Pilgrims were shooting Indians.

So I'm never quite sure why we eat turkey like everybody else.

"Hey, Dad," I said. "What do Indians have to be so thankful for?"

"We should give thanks that they didn't kill all of us."

We laughed like crazy. It was a good day. Dad was sober. Mom was getting ready to nap. Grandma was already napping.

But I missed Rowdy. I kept looking at the door. For the last ten years, he'd always come over to the house to have a pumpkin-pie eating contest with me.

I missed him.

So I drew a cartoon of Rowdy and me like we used to be:

Then I put on my coat and shoes, walked over to Rowdy's house, and knocked on the door.

Rowdy's dad, drunk as usual, opened the door.

"Junior," he said. "What do you want?"

"Is Rowdy home?"

"Nope."

"Oh, well, I drew this for him. Can you give it to him?"

Rowdy's dad took the cartoon and stared at it for a while. Then he smirked.

"You're kind of gay, aren't you?" he asked.

Yeah, that was the guy who was raising Rowdy. Jesus, no wonder my best friend was always so angry.

"Can you just give it to him?" I asked.

"Yeah, I'll give it to him. Even if it's a little gay."

I wanted to cuss at him. I wanted to tell him that I thought I was being courageous, and that I was trying to fix my broken friendship with Rowdy, and that I missed him, and if that was gay, then okay, I was the gayest dude in the world. But I didn't say any of that.

"Okay, thank you," I said instead. "And Happy Thanksgiving."

Rowdy's dad closed the door on me. I walked away. But I stopped at the end of the driveway and looked back. I could see Rowdy in the window of his upstairs bedroom. He was holding my cartoon. He was watching me walk away. And I could see the sadness in his face. I just *knew* he missed me, too.

I waved at him. He gave me the finger.

"Hey, Rowdy!" I shouted. "Thanks a lot!"

He stepped away from the window. And I felt sad for a moment. But then I realized that Rowdy may have flipped me off, but he hadn't torn up my cartoon. As much as he hated me, he probably should have ripped it to pieces. That would have hurt my feelings more than just about anything I can think of. But Rowdy still respected my cartoons. And so maybe he still respected me a little bit.

Hunger Pains

✳

Our history teacher, Mr. Sheridan, was trying to teach us something about the Civil War. But he was so boring and monotonous that he was only teaching us how to sleep with our eyes open.

I had to get out of there, so I raised my hand.

"What is it, Arnold?" the teacher asked.

"I have to go the bathroom."

"Hold it."

"I can't."

I put on my best If-I-Don't-Go-Now-I'm-Going-To-Explode face.

"Do you really have to?" the teacher asked.

I didn't have to go at first, but then I realized that yes, I did have to go.

"I have to go really bad," I said.

"All right, all right, go, go."

I headed over to the library bathrooms because they're usually a lot cleaner than the ones by the lunchroom.

So, okay, I'm going number two, and I'm sitting on the toilet, and I'm concentrating. I'm in my Zen mode, trying to make this whole thing a spiritual experience. I read once that Gandhi was way into his own number two. I don't know if he told fortunes or anything. But I guess he thought the condition and quality of his number two revealed the condition and quality of his life.

Yeah, I know, I probably read too many books.

And probably WAY too many books about number two.

But it's all important, okay? So I finish, flush, wash my hands, and then stare in the mirror and start popping zits. I'm all quiet and concentrating when I hear this weird noise coming from the other side of the wall.

That's the girls' bathroom.

And I hear that weird noise again.

Do you want to know what it sounds like?

It sounds like this:

ARGGHHHHHHHHSSSSSPPPPPPGGGHHHHHHH AAAAAARGHHHHHHHHHHAGGGGHH!

It sounds like somebody is vomiting.

Nope.

It sounds like a 747 is landing on a runway of vomit.

I'm planning on heading back to the classroom for more

scintillating lessons from the history teacher. But then I hear that noise again.

ARGGGHHHHHHHHSGHHSLLLSKSSSHHSDKFD JSABCDEFGHIJKLMNOPQRSTUVWXYZ!

Okay, so somebody might have the flu or something. Maybe they're having, like, kidney failure in there. I can't walk away.

So I knock on the door. The girls' bathroom door.

"Hey," I say. "Are you okay in there?"

"Go away!"

It's a girl, which makes sense, since it is the girls' bathroom.

"Do you want me to get a teacher or something?" I ask through the bathroom door.

"I said, GO AWAY!"

I'm not dumb. I can pick up on subtle clues.

So I walk away, but something pulls me back. I don't know what it is. If you're romantic, you might think it was destiny.

So destiny and me lean against the wall and wait.

The vomiter will eventually have to come out of the bathroom, and then I'll know that she's okay.

And pretty soon, she does come out.

And it is the lovely Penelope, and she's chomping hard on cinnamon gum. She'd obviously tried to cover the smell of vomit with the biggest piece of cinnamon gum in the world. But it doesn't work. She just smells like somebody vomited on a big old cinnamon tree.

"What are you looking at?" she asks me.

"I'm looking at an anorexic," I say.

A really HOT anorexic, I want to add, but I don't.

"I'm not anorexic," she says. "I'm bulimic."

She says it with her nose and chin in the air. She gets all

arrogant. And then I remember there are a bunch of anorexics who are PROUD to be skinny and starved freaks.

They think being anorexic makes them special, makes them better than everybody else. They have their own fricking Web sites where they give advice on the best laxatives and stuff.

"What's the difference between bulimics and anorexics?" I ask.

"Anorexics are anorexics all the time," she says. "I'm only bulimic when I'm throwing up."

Wow.

SHE SOUNDS JUST LIKE MY DAD!

There are all kinds of addicts, I guess. We all have pain. And we all look for ways to make the pain go away.

Penelope gorges on her pain and then throws it up and flushes it away. My dad drinks his pain away.

So I say to Penelope what I always say to Dad when he's drunk and depressed and ready to give up on the world.

"Hey, Penelope," I say. "Don't give up."

Okay, so it's not the wisest advice in the world. It's actually kind of obvious and corny.

But Penelope starts crying, talking about how lonely she is, and how everybody thinks her life is perfect because she's pretty and smart and popular, but that she's scared all the time, but nobody will let her be scared because she's pretty and smart and popular.

You notice that she mentioned her beauty, intelligence, and popularity twice in one sentence?

The girl has an ego.

But that's sexy, too.

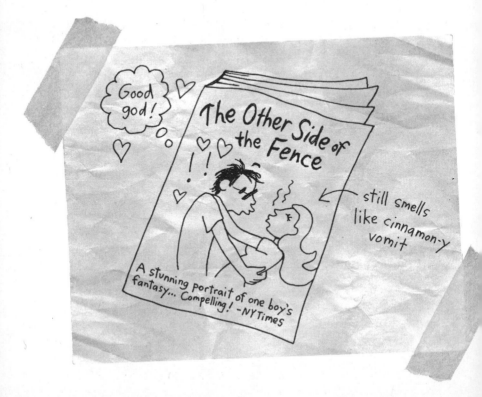

How is it that a bulimic girl with vomit on her breath can suddenly be so sexy? Love and lust can make you go crazy.

I suddenly understand how my big sister, Mary, could have met a guy and married him five minutes later. I'm not so mad at her for leaving us and moving to Montana.

Over the next few weeks, Penelope and I become the hot item at Reardan High School. Well, okay, we're not exactly a romantic couple. We're more like friends with potential. But that's still cool.

Everybody is absolutely shocked that Penelope chose me to be her new friend. I'm not some ugly, mutated beast. But I am an absolute stranger at the school.

And I am an Indian.

And Penelope's father, Earl, is a racist.

The first time I meet him, he said, "Kid, you better keep your hands out of my daughter's panties. She's only dating you because she knows it will piss me off. So I ain't going to get pissed. And if I ain't pissed then she'll stop dating you. In the meantime, you just keep your trouser snake in your trousers and I won't have to punch you in the stomach."

And then you know what he said to me after that?

"Kid, if you get my daughter pregnant, if you make some charcoal babies, I'm going to disown her. I'm going to kick her out of my house and you'll have to bring her home to your

BLEEEEATHPGH!

← Earl: #1 candidate for the Father-of-the-Year Award

slime

mommy and daddy. You hearing me straight, kid? This is all on you now."

Yep, Earl was a real winner.

Okay, so Penelope and I became the hot topic because we were defying the great and powerful Earl.

And, yeah, you're probably thinking that Penelope was dating me ONLY because I was the worst possible choice for her.

She was probably dating me ONLY because I was an Indian boy.

And, okay, so she was only semi-dating me. We held hands once in a while and we kissed once or twice, but that was it.

I don't know what I meant to her.

I think she was bored of being the prettiest, smartest, and most popular girl in the world. She wanted to get a little crazy, you know? She wanted to get a little smudged.

And I was the smudge.

But, hey, I was kind of using her, too.

After all, I suddenly became popular.

Because Penelope had publicly declared that I was cute enough to ALMOST date, all of the other girls in school decided that I was cute, too.

Because I got to hold hands with Penelope, and kiss her good-bye when she jumped on the school bus to go home, all of the other boys in school decided that I was a major stud.

Even the teachers started paying more attention to me.

I was mysterious.

How did I, the dorky Indian guy, win a tiny piece of Penelope's heart?

What was my secret?

I looked and talked and dreamed and walked differently than everybody else.

I was new.

If you want to get all biological, then you'd have to say that I was an exciting addition to the Reardan gene pool.

So, okay, those are all the obvious reasons why Penelope and I were friends. All the shallow reasons. But what about the bigger and better reasons?

"Arnold," she said one day after school, "I hate this little town. It's so small, too small. Everything about it is small. The people here have small ideas. Small dreams. They all want to marry each other and live here forever."

"What do you want to do?" I asked.

"I want to leave as soon as I can. I think I was born with a suitcase."

Yeah, she talked like that. All big and goofy and dramatic. I wanted to make fun of her, but she was so earnest.

"Where do you want to go?" I asked.

"Everywhere. I want to walk on the Great Wall of China. I want to walk to the top of pyramids in Egypt. I want to swim in every ocean. I want to climb Mount Everest. I want to go on an African safari. I want to ride a dogsled in Antarctica. I want all of it. Every single piece of everything."

Her eyes got this strange faraway look, like she'd been hypnotized.

I laughed.

"Don't laugh at me," she said.

"I'm not laughing at you," I said. "I'm laughing at your eyes."

"That's the whole problem," she said. "Nobody takes me seriously."

"Well, come on, it's kind of hard to take you seriously when you're talking about the Great Wall of China and Egypt and stuff. Those are just big goofy dreams. They're not real."

"They're real to me," she said.

"Why don't you quit talking in dreams and tell me what you really want to do with your life," I said. "Make it simple."

"I want to go to Stanford and study architecture."

"Wow, that's cool," I said. "But why architecture?"

"Because I want to build something beautiful. Because I want to be remembered."

And I couldn't make fun of her for that dream. It was my dream, too. And Indian boys weren't supposed to dream like that. And white girls from small towns weren't supposed to dream big, either.

We were supposed to be happy with our limitations. But there was no way Penelope and I were going to sit still. Nope, we both wanted to fly:

The ancillary tail feathers of the Australian tufted Arnelope makes this bird perfectly suited to long-distance flying at great altitudes.

"You know," I said. "I think it's way cool that you want to travel the world. But you won't even make it halfway if you don't eat enough."

She was in pain and I loved her, sort of loved her, I guess, so I kind of had to love her pain, too.

Mostly I loved to look at her. I guess that's what boys do, right? And men. We look at girls and women. We *stare* at them. And this is what I saw when I stared at Penelope:

Penelope
in her dad's old hat

Was it wrong to stare so much? Was it romantic at all? I don't know. But I couldn't help myself.

Maybe I don't know anything about romance, but I know a little bit about beauty.

And, man, Penelope was crazy beautiful.

Can you blame me for staring at her all day long?

Rowdy Gives Me Advice About Love

*

Have you ever watched a beautiful woman play volleyball?

Yesterday, during a game, Penelope was serving the ball and I watched her like she was a work of art.

She was wearing a white shirt and white shorts, and I could see the outlines of her white bra and white panties.

Her skin was pale white. Milky white. Cloud white.

So she was all white on white on white, like the most perfect kind of vanilla dessert cake you've ever seen.

I wanted to be her chocolate topping.

She was serving against the mean girls from Davenport Lady Gorillas. Yeah, you read that correctly. They willingly called themselves the Lady Gorillas. And they played like superstrong primates, too. Penelope and her teammates were getting killed. The score was like 12 to 0 in the first set.

But I didn't care.

I just wanted to watch the sweaty Penelope sweat her perfect sweat on that perfectly sweaty day.

She stood at the service line, bounced the volleyball a few times to get her rhythm, then tossed it into the air above her head.

She tracked the ball with her blue eyes. Just watched it intensely. Like that volleyball mattered more than anything else in the world. I got jealous of that ball. I wished I were that ball.

As the ball floated in the air, Penelope twisted her hips and back and swung her right arm back over her shoulder, coiling like a really pretty snake. Her leg muscles were stretched and taut.

I almost fainted when she served. Using all of that twisting and flexing and concentration, she smashed the ball and aced the Lady Gorillas.

And then Penelope clenched a fist and shouted, "Yes!"

Absolutely gorgeous.

Even though I didn't think I'd ever hear back, I wanted to know what to do with my feelings, so I walked over to the computer lab and e-mailed Rowdy. He's had the same address for five years.

"Hey, Rowdy," I wrote. "I'm in love with a white girl. What should I do?"

A few minutes later, Rowdy wrote back.

"Hey, Asshole," Rowdy wrote back. "I'm sick of Indian guys who treat white women like bowling trophies. Get a life."

Well, that didn't do me any good. So I asked Gordy what I should do about Penelope.

"I'm an Indian boy," I said. "How can I get a white girl to love me?"

"Let me do some research on that," Gordy said.

A few days later, he gave me a brief report.

"Hey, Arnold," he said. "I looked up 'in love with a white girl' on Google and found an article about that white girl named Cynthia who disappeared in Mexico last summer. You remember how her face was all over the papers and everybody said it was such a sad thing?"

"I kinda remember," I said.

"Well, this article said that over two hundred Mexican girls have disappeared in the last three years in that same part of the country. And nobody says much about that. And that's racist. The guy who wrote the article says people care more about beautiful white girls than they do about everybody else on the planet. White girls are privileged. They're damsels in distress."

"So what does that mean?" I asked.

"I think it means you're just a racist asshole like everybody else."

Wow.

In his own way, Gordy the bookworm was just as tough as Rowdy.

Gordy
(+ metaphysical boner)

Dance, Dance, Dance

✵

Traveling between Reardan and Wellpinit, between the little white town and the reservation, I always felt like a stranger.

I was half Indian in one place and half white in the other.

It was like being Indian was my job, but it was only a part-time job. And it didn't pay well at all.

The only person who made me feel great all the time was Penelope.

Well, I shouldn't say that.

I mean, my mother and father were working hard for me, too. They were constantly scraping together enough money to pay for gas, to get me lunch money, to buy me a new pair of jeans and a few new shirts.

My parents gave me just enough money so that I could pretend to have more money than I did.

I lied about how poor I was.

Everybody in Reardan assumed we Spokanes made lots of money because we had a casino. But that casino, mismanaged and too far away from major highways, was a money-losing business. In order to make money from the casino, you had to work at the casino.

And white people everywhere have always believed that the government just gives money to Indians.

And since the kids and parents at Reardan thought I had a lot of money, I did nothing to change their minds. I figured it wouldn't do me any good if they knew I was dirt poor.

What would they think of me if they knew I sometimes had to hitchhike to school?

Yeah, so I pretended to have a little money. I pretended to be middle class. I pretended I belonged.

Nobody knew the truth.

Of course, you can't lie forever. Lies have short shelf lives. Lies go bad. Lies rot and stink up the joint.

In December, I took Penelope to the Winter Formal. The thing is, I only had five dollars, not nearly enough to pay for anything — not for photos, not for food, not for gas, not for a hot dog and soda pop. If it had been any other dance, a regular dance, I would have stayed home with an imaginary illness. But I couldn't skip Winter Formal. And if I didn't take Penelope then she would have certainly gone with somebody else.

Because I didn't have money for gas, and because I couldn't have driven the car if I wanted to, and because I didn't want to double date, I told Penelope I'd meet her at the gym for the dance. She wasn't too happy about that.

But the worst thing is that I had to wear one of Dad's old suits:

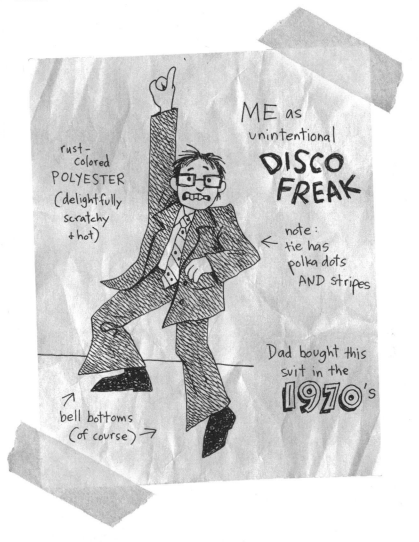

I was worried that people would make fun of me, right? And they probably would have if Penelope hadn't immediately squealed with delight when she first saw me walk into the gym.

"Oh, my, God!" she yelled for everybody to hear. "That suit is so beautiful. It's so retroactive. It's so retroactive that it's radioactive!"

And every dude in the joint immediately wished he'd worn his father's lame polyester suit.

And I imagined that every girl was immediately breathless and horny at the sight of my bell-bottom slacks.

So, drunk with my sudden power, I pulled off some lame disco dance moves that sent the place into hysterics.

Even Roger, the huge dude I'd punched in the face, was suddenly my buddy.

Penelope and I were so happy to be alive, and so happy to be alive TOGETHER, even if we were only a semi-hot item, and we danced every single dance.

Nineteen dances; nineteen songs.

Twelve fast songs; seven slow ones.

Eleven country hits; five rock songs; three hip-hop tunes.

It was the best night of my life.

Of course, I was a sweaty mess inside that hot polyester suit.

But it didn't matter. Penelope thought I was beautiful and so I felt beautiful.

And then the dance was over.

The lights flicked on.

And Penelope suddenly realized we'd forgotten to get our picture taken by the professional dude.

"Oh, my God!" she yelled. "We forgot to get our picture taken! That sucks!"

She was sad for a moment, but then she realized that she'd

had so much fun that a photograph of the evening was completely beside the point. A photograph would be just a lame souvenir.

I was completely relieved that we'd forgotten. I wouldn't have been able to pay for the photographs. I knew that. And I'd rehearsed a speech about losing my wallet.

I'd made it through the evening without revealing my poverty.

I figured I'd walk Penelope out to the parking lot, where her dad was waiting in his car. I'd give her a sweet little kiss on the cheek (because her dad would have shot me if I'd given her the tongue while he watched). And then I'd wave goodbye as they drove away. And then I'd wait in the parking lot until everybody was gone. And then I'd start the walk home in the dark. It was a Saturday, so I knew some reservation family would be returning home from Spokane. And I knew they'd see me and pick me up.

That was the plan.

But things changed. As things always change.

Roger and a few of the other dudes, the popular guys, decided they were going to drive into Spokane and have pancakes at some twenty-four–hour diner. It was suddenly the coolest idea in the world.

It was all seniors and juniors, upperclassmen, who were going together.

But Penelope was so popular, especially for a freshman, and I was popular by association, even as a freshman, too, that Roger invited us to come along.

Penelope was ecstatic about the idea.

I was sick to my stomach.

I had five bucks in my pocket. What could I buy with that? Maybe one plate of pancakes. Maybe.

I was doomed.

"What do you say, Arnie?" Roger asked. "You want to come carbo-load with us?"

"What do you want to do, Penelope?" I asked.

"Oh, I want to go, I want to go," she said. "Let me go ask Daddy."

Oh, man, I saw my only escape. I could only hope that Earl wouldn't let her go. Only Earl could save me now.

I was counting on Earl! That's how bad my life was at that particular moment!

Penelope skipped over toward her father's car.

"Hey, Penultimate," Roger said. "I'll go with you. I'll tell Earl you guys are riding with me. And I'll drive you guys home."

Roger's nickname for Penelope was Penultimate. It was maybe the biggest word he knew. I hated that he had a nickname for her. And as they walked together toward Earl, I realized that Roger and Penelope looked good together. They looked natural. They looked like they should be a couple.

And after they all found out I was a poor-ass Indian, I knew they would be a couple.

Come on, Earl! Come on, Earl! Break your daughter's heart!

But Earl loved Roger. Every dad loved Roger. He was the best football player they'd ever seen. Of course they loved him. It would have been un-American not to love the best football player.

I imagined that Earl said his daughter could go only if Roger got his hands into her panties instead of me.

I was angry and jealous and absolutely terrified.

"I can go! I can go!" Penelope said, ran back to me, and hugged me hard.

An hour later, about twenty of us were sitting in a Denny's in Spokane.

Everybody ordered pancakes.

I ordered pancakes for Penelope and me. I ordered orange juice and coffee and a side order of toast and hot chocolate and French fries, too, even though I knew I wouldn't be able to pay for any of it.

I figured it was my last meal before my execution, and I was going to have a feast.

Halfway through our meal, I went to the bathroom.

I thought maybe I was going to throw up, so I kneeled at the toilet. But I only retched a bit.

Roger came into the bathroom and heard me.

"Hey, Arnie," he said. "Are you okay?"

"Yeah," I said. "I'm just tired."

"All right, man," he said. "I'm happy you guys came tonight. You and Penultimate are a great couple, man."

"You think so?"

"Yeah, have you done her yet?"

"I don't really want to talk about that stuff."

"Yeah, you're right, dude. It's none of my business. Hey, man, are you going to try out for basketball?"

I knew that practice started in a week. I'd planned on playing. But I didn't know if the Coach liked Indians or not.

"Yeah," I said.

"Are you any good?"

"I'm okay."

"You think you're good enough to play varsity?" Roger asked.

"No way," I said. "I'm junior varsity all the way."

"All right," Roger said. "It will be good to have you out there. We need some new blood."

"Thanks, man," I said.

I couldn't believe he was so nice. He was, well, he was POLITE! How many great football players are polite? And kind? And generous like that?

It was amazing.

"Hey, listen," I said. "The reason I was getting sick in there is —"

I thought about telling him the whole truth, but I just couldn't.

"I bet you're just sick with love," Roger said.

"No, well, yeah, maybe," I said. "But the thing is, my stomach is all messed up because I, er, forgot my wallet. I left my money at home, man."

"Dude!" Roger said. "Man, don't sweat it. You should have said something earlier. I got you covered."

He opened his wallet and handed me forty bucks.

Holy, holy.

What kind of kid can just hand over forty bucks like that?

"I'll pay you back, man," I said.

"Whenever, man, just have a good time, all right?"

He slapped me on the back again. He was always slapping me on the back.

We walked back to the table together, finished our food, and Roger drove me back to the school. I told them my dad was going to pick me up outside the gym.

"Dude," Roger said. "It's three in the morning."

"It's okay," I said. "My dad works the swing shift. He's coming here straight from work."

"Are you sure?"

"Yeah, everything is cool."

"I'll bring Penultimate home safely, man."

"Cool."

So Penelope and I got out of the car so we could have a private good-bye. She had laser eyes.

"Roger told me he lent you some money," she said.

"Yeah," I said. "I forgot my wallet."

Her laser eyes grew hotter.

"Arnold?"

"Yeah?"

"Can I ask you something big?"

"Yeah, I guess."

"Are you poor?"

I couldn't lie to her anymore.

"Yes," I said. "I'm poor."

I figured she was going to march out of my life right then. But she didn't. Instead she kissed me. On the cheek. I guess poor guys don't get kissed on the lips. I was going to yell at her for being shallow. But then I realized that she was being my friend. Being a really good friend, in fact. She was concerned about me. I'd been thinking about her breasts and she'd been thinking about my whole life. I was the shallow one.

"Roger was the one who guessed you were poor," she said.

"Oh, great, now he's going to tell everybody."

"He's not going to tell anybody. Roger likes you. He's a great guy. He's like my big brother. He can be your friend, too."

That sounded pretty good to me. I needed friends more than I needed my lust-filled dreams.

"Is your Dad really coming to pick you up?" she asked.

"Yes," I said.

"Are you telling the truth?"

"No," I said.

"How will you get home?" she asked.

"Most nights, I walk home. I hitchhike. Somebody usually picks me up. I've only had to walk the whole way a few times."

She started to cry.

FOR ME!

Who knew that tears of sympathy could be so sexy?

"Oh, my God, Arnold, you can't do that," she said. "I won't let you do that. You'll freeze. Roger will drive you home. He'll be happy to drive you home."

I tried to stop her, but Penelope ran over to Roger's car and told him the truth.

And Roger, being of kind heart and generous pocket, and a little bit racist, drove me home that night.

And he drove me home plenty of other nights, too.

If you let people into your life a little bit, they can be pretty damn amazing.

Don't Trust
Your
Computer
✳

Today at school, I was really missing Rowdy, so I walked over to the computer lab, took a digital photo of my smiling face, and e-mailed it to him.

A few minutes later, he e-mailed me a digital photo of his bare ass. I don't know when he snapped that pic.

It made me laugh.

And it made me depressed, too.

Rowdy could be so crazy-funny-disgusting. The Reardan kids were so worried about grades and sports and THEIR FUTURES that they sometimes acted like repressed middle-aged business dudes with cell phones stuck in their small intestines.

Rowdy was the opposite of repressed. He was exactly the kind of kid who would e-mail his bare ass (and bare everything else) to the world.

"Hey," Gordy said. "Is that somebody's posterior?"

Posterior! Did he just say "posterior"?

"Gordy, my man," I said. "That is most definitely NOT a posterior. That is a stinky ass. You can smell the thing, even through the computer."

"Whose butt is that?" he asked.

"Ah, it's my best friend, Rowdy. Well, he used to be my best friend. He hates me now."

"How come he hates you?" he asked.

"Because I left the rez," I said.

"But you still live there, don't you? You're just going to school here."

"I know, I know, but some Indians think you have to act white to make your life better. Some Indians think you *become* white if you try to make your life better, if you become successful."

"If that were true, then wouldn't all white people be successful?"

Man, Gordy was smart. I wished I could take him to the rez and let him educate Rowdy. Of course, Rowdy would probably punch Gordy until he was brain-dead. Or maybe Rowdy, Gordy, and I could become a superhero trio, fighting for truth, justice, and the Native American way. Well, okay, Gordy was white, but anybody can start to act like an Indian if he hangs around us long enough.

"The people at home," I said. "A lot of them call me an apple."

"Do they think you're a fruit or something?" he asked.

"No, no," I said. "They call me an apple because they think I'm red on the outside and white on the inside."

"Ah, so they think you're a traitor."

"Yep."

"Well, life is a constant struggle between being an individual and being a member of the community."

Can you believe there is a kid who talks like that? Like he's already a college professor impressed with the sound of his own voice?

"Gordy," I said. "I don't understand what you're trying to say to me."

"Well, in the early days of humans, the community was our only protection against predators, and against starvation. We survived because we trusted one another."

"So?"

"So, back in the day, weird people threatened the strength of the tribe. If you weren't good for making food, shelter, or babies, then you were tossed out on your own."

"But we're not primitive like that anymore."

"Oh, yes, we are. Weird people still get banished."

"You mean weird people like me," I said.

"And me," Gordy said.

"All right, then," I said. "So we have a tribe of two."

I had the sudden urge to hug Gordy, and he had the sudden urge to prevent me from hugging him.

"Don't get sentimental," he said.

Yep, even the weird boys are afraid of their emotions.

My Sister
Sends Me
a Letter

Dear Junior,

I am still looking for a job. They keep telling
me I don't have enough experience. But how
can I get enough experience if they don't give
me a chance to get experience? Oh, well. I have
a lot of free time, so I have started to write my
life story. Really! Isn't that crazy? I think I'm
going to call it HOW TO RUN AWAY FROM YOUR
HOUSE AND FIND YOUR HOME.

What do you think?

Tell everybody I love them and miss them!

Love,
your Big Sis!

P.S.
And we moved into a new house.
It's the most gorgeous place in the world!

From a photo she sent of her "gorgeous new place."

Looks like a TV dinner tray.

Reindeer Games

*

I almost didn't try out for the Reardan basketball team. I just figured I wasn't going to be good enough to make even the C squad. And I didn't want to get cut from the team. I didn't think I could live through that humiliation.

But my dad changed my mind.

"Do you know about the first time I met your mother?" he asked.

"You're both from the rez," I said. "So it was on the rez. Big duh."

"But I only moved to this rez when I was five years old."

"So."

"So your mother is eight years older than me."

"And there's a partridge in the pear tree. Get to the point, Dad."

"Your mother was thirteen and I was five when we first met. And guess how we first met?"

"How?"

"She helped me get a drink from a water fountain."

"Well, that just seems sort of gross," I said.

"I was tiny," Dad said. "And she boosted me up so I could get a drink. And imagine, all these years later and we're married and have two kids."

"What does this have to do with basketball?"

"You have to dream big to get big."

"That's pretty dang optimistic for you, Dad."

"Well, you know, your mother helped me get a drink from the water fountain last night, if you know what I mean."

And all I could say to my father was, "Ewwwww-wwwww."

That's one more thing people don't know about Indians: we love to talk dirty.

Anyway, I signed up for basketball.

On the first day of practice, I stepped onto the court and felt short, skinny, and slow.

All of the white boys were good. Some were great.

I mean, there were some guys who were 6 foot 6 and 6 foot 7.

Roger the Giant was strong and fast and could dunk.

I tried to stay out of way. I figured I'd die if he ran me over. But he just smiled all the time, played hard, and slapped me hard on the back.

We all shot basketballs for a while. And then Coach stepped onto the court.

Forty kids IMMEDIATELY stopped bouncing and shoot-ing and talking. We were silent, SNAP, just like that.

"I want to thank you all for coming out today," Coach said.

"There are forty of you. But we only have room for twelve on the varsity and twelve on the junior varsity."

I knew I wouldn't make those teams. I was C squad material, for sure.

"In other years, we've also had a twelve-man C squad," Coach said. "But we don't have the budget for it this year. That means I'm going to have to cut sixteen players today."

Twenty boys puffed up their chests. They knew they were good enough to make either the varsity or the junior varsity.

The other twenty shook their heads. We knew we were cuttable.

"I really hate to do this," Coach said. "If it were up to me, I'd keep everybody. But it's not up to me. So we're just going to have to do our best here, okay? You play with dignity and respect, and I'll treat you with dignity and respect, no matter what happens, okay?"

We all agreed to that.

"Okay, let's get started," Coach said.

The first drill was a marathon. Well, not exactly a marathon. We had to run one hundred laps around the gym. So forty of us ran.

And thirty-six of us finished.

After fifty laps, one guy quit, and since quitting is contagious, three other boys caught the disease and walked off the court, too.

No can do.

The Eimouttaheer Virus

I didn't understand. Why would you try out for a basketball team if you didn't want to run?

I didn't mind. After all, that meant only twelve more guys had to be cut. I only had to be better than twelve other guys.

Well, we were good and tired after that run.

And then Coach immediately had us playing full-court one-on-one.

That's right.

FULL-COURT ONE-ON-ONE.

That was torture.

Coach didn't break it down by position. So quick guards had to guard power forwards, and vice versa. Seniors had to guard freshmen, and vice versa. All-stars had to guard losers like me, and vice versa.

Coach threw me the ball and said, "Go."

So I turned and dribbled straight down the court.

A mistake.

Roger easily poked the ball away and raced down toward his basket.

Ashamed, I was frozen.

"What are you waiting for?" Coach asked me. "Play some D."

Awake, I ran after Roger, but he dunked it before I was even close.

"Go again," Coach said.

This time, Roger tried to dribble down the court. And I played defense. I crouched down low, spread my arms and legs high and wide, and gritted my teeth.

And then Roger ran me over. Just sent me sprawling.

He raced down and dunked it again while I lay still on the floor.

Coach walked over and looked down at me.

"What's your name, kid?" he asked.

"Arnold," I said.

"You're from the reservation?"

"Yes."

"Did you play basketball up there?"

"Yes. For the eighth-grade team."

Coach studied my face.

"I remember you," he said. "You were a good shooter."

"Yeah," I said.

Coach studied my face some more, as if he were searching for something.

"Roger is a big kid," he said.

"He's huge," I said.

"You want to take him on again? Or do you need a break?"

Ninety percent of me wanted to take the break. But I knew if I took that break I would never make the team.

"I'll take him on again," I said.

Coach smiled.

"All right, Roger," he said. "Line up again."

I stood up again. Coach threw me the ball. And Roger came for me. He screamed and laughed like a crazy man. He was having a great time. And he was trying to intimidate me.

He did intimidate me.

I dribbled with my right hand toward Roger, knowing that he was going to try to steal the ball.

If he stayed in front of me and reached for the ball with his left hand, then there was no way I could get past him. He was too big and strong, too immovable. But he reached for the ball with his right hand, and that put him a little off balance, so I spun-dribbled around him, did a 360, and raced down the court. He was right behind me. I thought I could outrun him, but he caught up to me and just blasted me. Just me skidding across the floor again. The ball went bouncing into the stands.

I should have stayed down.

But I didn't.

Instead, I jumped up, ran into the stands, grabbed the loose ball, and raced toward Roger standing beneath the basket.

I didn't even dribble.

I just ran like a fullback.

Roger crouched, ready to tackle me like he was a middle linebacker.

He screamed; I screamed.

And then I stopped short, about fifteen feet from the hoop, and made a pretty little jump shot.

Everybody in the gym yelled and clapped and stomped their feet.

Roger was mad at first, but then he smiled, grabbed the ball, and dribbled toward his hoop.

He spun left, right, but I stayed with him.

He bumped me, pushed me, and elbowed me, but I stayed with him. He went up for a layup and I fouled him. But I'd learned there are NO FOULS CALLED IN FULL-COURT ONE-ON-ONE, so I grabbed the loose ball and raced for my end again.

But Coach blew the whistle.

"All right, all right, Arnold, Roger," Coach said. "That's good, that's good. Next two, next two."

I took my place at the back of the line and Roger stood next to me.

"Good job," he said and offered his fist.

I bumped his fist with mine. I was a warrior!

And that's when I knew I was going to make the team.

Heck, I ended up on the varsity. As a freshman. Coach said I was the best shooter who'd ever played for him. And I was going to be his secret weapon. I was going to be his Weapon of Mass Destruction.

Coach sure loved those military metaphors.

Two weeks later, we traveled up the road for our first game of the season. And our first game was against Wellpinit High School.

Yep.

It was like something out of Shakespeare.

The morning of the game, I'd woken up in my rez house, so my dad could drive me the twenty-two miles to Reardan, so I could get on the team bus for the ride back to the reservation.

Crazy.

Do I have to tell you that I was absolutely sick with fear?

I vomited four times that day.

When our bus pulled into the high school parking lot, we were greeted by some rabid elementary school kids. Some of those little dudes and dudettes were my cousins.

They pelted our bus with snowballs. And some of those snowballs were filled with rocks.

As we got off the bus and walked toward the gym, I could hear the crowd going crazy inside.

They were chanting something.

I couldn't make it out.

And then I could.

The rez basketball fans were chanting, "Ar-nold sucks! Ar-nold sucks! Ar-nold sucks!"

They weren't calling me by my rez name, Junior. Nope, they were calling me by my Reardan name.

I stopped.

Coach looked back at me.

"Are you okay?" he asked.

"No," I said.

"You don't have to play this one," he said.

"Yes, I do," I said.

Still, I probably would have turned around if I hadn't seen my mom and dad and grandma waiting at the front door.

I know they'd been pitched just as much crap as I was. And there they were, ready to catch more crap for me. Ready to walk through the crap with me.

Two tribal cops were also there.

I guess they were for security. For whose security, I don't know. But they walked with our team, too.

So we walked through the front and into the loud gym.

Which immediately went silent.

Absolutely quiet.

My fellow tribal members saw me and they all stopped cheering, talking, and moving.

I think they stopped breathing.

And, then, as one, they all turned their backs on me.

It was a fricking awesome display of contempt.

I was impressed. So were my teammates.

Especially Roger.

He just looked at me and whistled.

I was mad.

If these dang Indians had been this organized when I went to school here, maybe I would have had more reasons to stay.

That thought made me laugh.

So I laughed.

And my laughter was the only sound in the gym.

And then I noticed that the only Indian who hadn't turned his back on me was Rowdy. He was standing on the other end of the court. He passed a basketball around his back, around his back, around his back, like a clock. And he glared at me.

He wanted to play.

He didn't want to turn his back on me.

He wanted to kill me, face-to-face.

That made me laugh some more.

And then Coach started laughing with me.

And so did my teammates.

And we kept laughing as we walked into the locker room to get ready for the game.

Once inside the locker room, I almost passed out. I slumped against a locker. I felt dizzy and weak. And then I cried, and felt ashamed of my tears.

But Coach knew exactly what to say.

"It's okay," Coach said to me, but he was talking to the whole team. "If you care about something enough, it's going to make you cry. But you have to use it. Use your tears. Use your pain. Use your fear. Get mad, Arnold, get mad."

And so I got mad.

And I was still mad and crying when we ran out for warm-ups. And I was still mad when the game started. I was on the bench. I didn't think I was going to play much. I was only a freshman.

But halfway through the first quarter, with the score tied at 10, Coach sent me in.

And as I ran onto the court, somebody in the crowd threw a quarter at me. AND HIT ME IN THE FRICKING FOREHEAD!

They drew blood.

I was bleeding. So I couldn't play.

Bleeding and angry, I glared at the crowd.

They taunted me as I walked into the locker room.

I bled alone, until Eugene, my dad's best friend, walked in. He had just become an EMT for the tribal clinic.

"Let me look at that," he said, and poked at my wound.

"You still got your motorcycle?" I asked.

"Nah, I wrecked that thing," he said, and dabbed antiseptic on my cut. "How does this feel?"

"It hurts."

"Ah, it's nothing," he said. "Maybe three stitches. I'll drive you to Spokane to get it fixed up."

"Do you hate me, too?" I asked Eugene.

"No, man, you're cool," he said.

"Good," I said.

"It's too bad you didn't get to play," Eugene said. "Your dad says you're getting pretty good."

"Not as good as you," I said.

Eugene was a legend. People say he could have played in college, but people also say Eugene couldn't read.

You can't read, you can't ball.

"You'll get them next time," Eugene said.

"You stitch me up," I said.

"What?"

"You stitch me up. I want to play tonight."

"I can't do that, man. It's your face. I might leave a scar or something."

"Then I'll look tougher," I said. "Come on, man."

So Eugene did it. He gave me three stitches in my forehead and it hurt like crazy, but I was ready to play the second half.

We were down by five points.

Rowdy had been an absolute terror, scoring twenty points, grabbing ten rebounds, and stealing the ball seven times.

"That kid is good," Coach said.

"He's my best friend," I said. "Well, he used to be my best friend."

"What is he now?"

"I don't know."

We scored the first five points of the third quarter, and then Coach sent me into the game.

I immediately stole a pass and drove for a layup.

Rowdy was right behind me.

I jumped into the air, heard the curses of two hundred Spokanes, and then saw only a bright light as Rowdy smashed his elbow into my head and knocked me unconscious.

Okay, I don't remember anything else from that night. So everything I tell you now is secondhand information.

After Rowdy knocked me out, both of our teams got into a series of shoving matches and push-fights.

The tribal cops had to pull twenty or thirty adult Spokanes off the court before any of them assaulted a teenage white kid.

Rowdy was given a technical foul.

So we shot two free throws for that.

I didn't shoot them, of course, because I was already in Eugene's ambulance, with my mother and father, on the way to Spokane.

After we shot the technical free throws, the two referees huddled. They were two white dudes from Spokane who were absolutely terrified of the wild Indians in the crowd and were willing to do ANYTHING to make them happy. So they called technical fouls on four of our players for leaving the bench and on Coach for unsportsmanlike conduct.

Yep, five technicals. Ten free throws.

After Rowdy hit the first six free throws, Coach cursed and screamed, and was thrown out of the game.

Wellpinit ended up winning by thirty points.

I ended up with a minor concussion.

Yep, three stitches and a bruised brain.

My mother was just beside herself. She thought I'd been murdered.

"I'm okay," I said. "Just a little dizzy."

"But your hydrocephalus," she said. "Your brain is already damaged enough."

"Gee, thanks, Mom," I said.

Of course, I was worried that I'd further damaged my already damaged brain; the doctors said I was fine.

Mostly fine.

Later that night, Coach talked his way past the nurses and into my room. My mother and father and grandma were asleep in their chairs, but I was awake.

"Hey, kid," Coach said, keeping his voice low so he wouldn't wake my family.

"Hey, Coach," I said.

"Sorry about that game," he said.

"It's not your fault."

"I shouldn't have played you. I should have canceled the whole game. It's my fault."

"I wanted to play. I wanted to win."

"It's just a game," he said. "It's not worth all this."

But he was lying. He was just saying what he thought he was supposed to say. Of course, it was not just a game. Every game is important. Every game is serious.

"Coach," I said. "I would walk out of this hospital and walk all the way back to Wellpinit to play them right now if I could."

Coach smiled.

"Vince Lombardi used to say something I like," he said.

"It's not whether you win or lose," I said. "It's how you play the game."

"No, but I like that one," Coach said. "But Lombardi didn't mean it. Of course, it's better to win."

We laughed.

"No, I like this other one more," Coach said. "The quality of a man's life is in direct proportion to his commitment to excellence, regardless of his chosen field of endeavor."

"That's a good one."

"It's perfect for you. I've never met anybody as committed as you."

"Thanks, Coach."

"You're welcome. Okay, kid, you take care of your head. I'm going to get out of here so you can sleep."

"Oh, I'm not supposed to sleep. They want to keep me awake to monitor my head. Make sure I don't have some hidden damage or something."

"Oh, okay," Coach said. "Well, how about I stay and keep you company, then?"

"Wow, that would be great."
So Coach and I sat awake all night.
We told each other many stories.
But I never repeat those stories.
That night belongs to just me and my coach.

And a Partridge in a Pear Tree

✳

When the holidays rolled around, we didn't have any money for presents, so Dad did what he always does when we don't have enough money.

He took what little money we did have and ran away to get drunk.

He left on Christmas Eve and came back on January 2.

With an epic hangover, he just lay on his bed for hours.

"Hey, Dad," I said.

"Hey, kid," he said. "I'm sorry about Christmas."

"It's okay," I said.

But it wasn't okay. It was about as far from okay as you can get. If okay was the earth, then I was standing on Jupiter. I don't know why I said it was okay. For some reason, I was protecting the feelings of the man who had broken my heart yet again.

Jeez, I'd just won the Silver Medal in the Children of Alcoholics Olympics.

"I got you something," he said.

"What?"

"It's in my boot."

I picked up one of his cowboy boots.

"No, the other one," he said. "Inside, under that foot-pad thing."

I picked up the other boot and dug inside. Man, that thing smelled like booze and fear and failure.

I found a wrinkled and damp five dollar bill.

"Merry Christmas," he said.

Wow.

Drunk for a week, my father must have really wanted to spend those last five dollars. Shoot, you can buy a bottle of the worst whiskey for five dollars. He could have spent that five bucks and stayed drunk for another day or two. But he saved it for me.

It was a beautiful and ugly thing.

"Thanks, Dad," I said.

He was asleep.

"Merry Christmas," I said, and kissed him on the cheek.

Red Versus
White
✳

You probably think I've completely fallen in love with white people and that I don't see anything good in Indians.

Well, that's false.

I love my big sister. I think she's double crazy and random.

Ever since she moved, she's sent me all these great Montana postcards. Beautiful landscapes and beautiful Indians. Buffalo. Rivers. Huge insects.

Great postcards.

She still can't find a job, and she's still living in that crappy little trailer. But she's happy and working hard on her book. She made a New Year's resolution to finish her book by summertime.

Her book is about hope, I guess.

I think she wants me to share in her romance.

I love her for that.

And I love my mother and father and my grandma.

Ever since I've been at Reardan, and seen how great parents do their great parenting, I realize that my folks are pretty good. Sure, my dad has a drinking problem and my mom can be a little eccentric, but they make sacrifices for me. They worry about me. They talk to me. And best of all, they listen to me.

I've learned that the worst thing a parent can do is ignore their children.

And, trust me, there are plenty of Reardan kids who get ignored by their parents.

There are white parents, especially fathers, who never come to the school. They don't come for their kids' games, concerts, plays, or carnivals.

I'm friends with some white kids, and I've never met their fathers.

That's absolutely freaky.

On the rez, you know every kid's father, mother, grandparents, dog, cat, and shoe size. I mean, yeah, Indians are screwed up, but we're really close to each other. We KNOW each other. Everybody knows everybody.

But despite the fact that Reardan is a tiny town, people can still be strangers to each other.

I've learned that white people, especially fathers, are good at hiding in plain sight.

I mean, yeah, my dad would sometimes go on a drinking binge and be gone for a week, but those white dads can completely disappear without ever leaving the living room.

They can just BLEND into their chairs. They become their chairs.

So, okay, I'm not all goofy-eyed in love with white people, all right? Plenty of the old white guys still give me the stink eye just for being Indian. And a lot of them think I shouldn't be in the school at all.

I'm realistic, okay?

I've thought about these things. And maybe I haven't done enough thinking, but I've done enough to know that it's better to live in Reardan than in Wellpinit.

Maybe only slightly better.

But from where I'm standing, slightly better is about the size of the Grand Canyon.

And, hey, do you want to know the very best thing about Reardan?

It's Penelope, of course. And maybe Gordy.

And do you want to know what the very best thing was about Wellpinit?

My grandmother.

She was amazing.

She was the most amazing person in the world.

Do you want to know the very best thing about my grandmother?

She was tolerant.

And I know that's a hilarious thing to say about your grandmother.

I mean, when people compliment their grandmothers, especially their Indian grandmothers, they usually say things like, "My grandmother is so wise" and "My grandmother is so kind" and "My grandmother has seen everything."

And, yeah, my grandmother was smart and kind and had traveled to about 100 different Indian reservations, but that had nothing to do with her greatness.

My grandmother's greatest gift was tolerance.

Now, in the old days, Indians used to be forgiving of any kind of eccentricity. In fact, weird people were often celebrated.

Epileptics were often shamans because people just assumed that God gave seizure-visions to the lucky ones.

Gay people were seen as magical, too.

I mean, like in many cultures, men were viewed as warriors and women were viewed as caregivers. But gay people, being both male and female, were seen as both warriors and caregivers.

Gay people could do anything. They were like Swiss Army knives!

My grandmother had no use for all the gay bashing and homophobia in the world, especially among other Indians.

"Jeez," she said. "Who cares if a man wants to marry another man? All I want to know is who's going to pick up all the dirty socks?"

Of course, ever since white people showed up and brought along their Christianity and their fears of eccentricity, Indians have gradually lost all of their tolerance.

Indians can be just as judgmental and hateful as any white person.

But not my grandmother.

She still hung on to that old-time Indian spirit, you know?

She always approached each new person and each new experience the exact same way.

Whenever we went to Spokane, my grandmother would talk to anybody, even the homeless people, even the homeless guys who were talking to invisible people.

My grandmother would start talking to the invisible people, too.

Why would she do that?

"Well," she said, "how can I be sure there aren't invisible

people in the world? Scientists didn't believe in the mountain gorilla for hundreds of years. And now look. So if scientists can be wrong, then all of us can be wrong. I mean, what if all of those invisible people ARE scientists? Think about that one."

So I thought about that one:

Invisible Mountain Gorilla Scientist

After I decided to go to Reardan, I felt like an invisible mountain gorilla scientist. My grandmother was the only one who thought it was a 100 percent good idea.

"Think of all the new people you're going to meet," she said. "That's the whole point of life, you know? To meet new people. I wish I could go with you. It's such an exciting idea."

Of course, my grandmother had met thousands, tens of thousands, of other Indians at powwows all over the country. Every powwow Indian knew her.

Yep, my grandmother was powwow-famous.

Everybody loved her; she loved everybody.

In fact, last week, she was walking back home from a mini powwow at the Spokane Tribal Community Center, when she was struck and killed by a drunk driver.

Yeah, you read that right.

She didn't die right away. The reservation paramedics kept her alive long enough to get to the hospital in Spokane, but she died during emergency surgery.

Massive internal injuries.

At the hospital, my mother wept and wailed. She'd lost her mother. When anybody, no matter how old they are, loses a parent, I think it hurts the same as if you were only five years old, you know? I think all of us are always five years old in the presence and absence of our parents.

My father was all quiet and serious with the surgeon, a big and handsome white guy.

"Did she say anything before she died?" he asked.

"Yes," the surgeon said. "She said, 'Forgive him.'"

"Forgive him?" my father asked.

"I think she was referring to the drunk driver who killed her."

Wow.

My grandmother's last act on earth was a call for forgiveness, love, and tolerance.

She wanted us to forgive Gerald, the dumb-ass Spokane Indian alcoholic who ran her over and killed her.

I think my dad wanted to go find Gerald and beat him to death.

I think my mother would have helped him.

I think I would have helped him, too.

But my grandmother wanted us to forgive her murderer.

Even dead, she was a better person than us.

The tribal cops found Gerald hiding out at Benjamin Lake.
They took him to jail.

And after we got back from the hospital, my father went over to see Gerald to kill him or forgive him. I think the tribal cops might have looked the other way if my father had decided to strangle Gerald.

But my father, respecting my grandmother's last wishes, left Gerald alone to the justice system, which ended up sending him to prison for eighteen months. After he got out, Gerald moved to a reservation in California and nobody ever saw him again.

But my family had to bury my grandmother.

I mean, it's natural to bury your grandmother.

Grandparents are supposed to die first, but they're supposed to die of old age. They're supposed to die of a heart attack or a stroke or of cancer or of Alzheimer's.

THEY ARE NOT SUPPOSED TO GET RUN OVER AND KILLED BY A DRUNK DRIVER!

I mean, the thing is, plenty of Indians have died because they were drunk. And plenty of drunken Indians have killed other drunken Indians.

But my grandmother had never drunk alcohol in her life. Not one drop. That's the rarest kind of Indian in the world.

I know only, like, five Indians in our whole tribe who have never drunk alcohol.

And my grandmother was one of them.

"Drinking would shut down my seeing and my hearing and my feeling," she used to say. "Why would I want to be in the world if I couldn't touch the world with all of my senses intact?"

Well, my grandmother has left this world and she's now roaming around the afterlife.

Wake

We held Grandmother's wake three days later. We knew that people would be coming in large numbers. But we were stunned because almost two thousand Indians showed up that day to say good-bye.

And nobody gave me any crap.

I mean, I was still the kid who had betrayed the tribe. And that couldn't be forgiven. But I was also the kid who'd lost his grandmother. And everybody knew that losing my grandmother was horrible. So they all waved the white flag that day and let me grieve in peace.

And after that, they stopped hassling me whenever they saw me on the rez. I mean, I still lived on the rez, right? And I had to go get the mail and get milk from the trading post and just hang out, right? So I was still a part of the rez.

People had either ignored me or called me names or pushed me.

But they stopped after my grandmother died.

I guess they realized that I was in enough pain already. Or maybe they realized they'd been cruel jerks.

I wasn't suddenly popular, of course. But I wasn't a villain anymore.

No matter what else happened between my tribe and me, I would always love them for giving me peace on the day of my grandmother's funeral.

Even Rowdy just stood far away.

He would always be my best friend, no matter how much he hated me.

We had to move the coffin out of the Spokane Tribal Longhouse and set it on the fifty-yard line of the football field.

We were lucky the weather was good.

Yep, about two thousand Indians (and a few white folks) sat and stood on the football field as we all said good-bye to the greatest Spokane Indian in history.

I knew that my grandmother would have loved that send-off.

It was crazy and fun and sad.

My sister wasn't able to come to the funeral. That was the worst part about it. She didn't have enough money to get back, I guess. That was sad. But she promised me she'd sing one hundred mourning songs that day.

We all have to find our own ways to say good-bye.

Tons of people told stories about my grandmother.

But there was one story that mattered most of all.

About ten hours into the wake, a white guy stood. He was a stranger. He looked vaguely familiar. I knew I'd seen him before, but I couldn't think of where. We all wondered exactly who he was. But nobody knew. That wasn't surprising. My grandmother had met thousands of people.

The white guy was holding this big suitcase.

He held that thing tight to his chest as he talked.

"Hello," he said. "My name is Ted."

And then I remembered who he was. He was a rich and famous billionaire white dude. He was famous for being filthy rich and really weird.

My grandmother knew Billionaire Ted!

Wow.

We all were excited to hear this guy's story. And so what did he have to say?

We all groaned.

We'd expected this white guy to be original. But he was yet another white guy who showed up on the rez because he loved Indian people SOOOOOOO much.

Do you know how many white strangers show up on Indian reservations every year and start telling Indians how much they love them?

Thousands.

It's sickening.

And boring.

"Listen," Ted said. "I know you've heard that before. I know white people say that all the time. But I still need to say it. I love Indians. I love your songs, your dances, and your souls. And I love your art. I collect Indian art."

Oh, God, he was a collector. Those guys made Indians feel like insects pinned to a display board. I looked around the football field. Yep, all of my cousins were squirming like beetles and butterflies with pins stuck in their hearts.

"I've collected Indian art for decades," Ted said. "I have old spears. Old arrowheads. I have old armor. I have blankets. And paintings. And sculptures. And baskets. And jewelry."

Blah, blah, blah, blah.

"And I have old powwow dance outfits," he said.

Now that made everybody sit up and pay attention.

"About ten years ago, this Indian guy knocked on the door of my cabin in Montana."

Cabin, my butt. Ted lived in a forty-room log mansion just outside of Bozeman.

"Well, I didn't know this stranger," Ted said. "But I always open my door to Indians."

Oh, please.

"And this particular Indian stranger was holding a very beautiful powwow dance outfit, a woman's powwow dance outfit. It was the most beautiful thing I'd ever seen. It was all beaded blue and red and yellow with a thunderbird design. It must have weighed fifty pounds. And I couldn't imagine the strength of the woman who could dance beneath that magical burden."

Every woman in the world could dance that way.

"Well, this Indian stranger said he was in a desperate situation. His wife was dying of cancer and he needed money to pay for her medicine. I knew he was lying. I knew he'd stolen the outfit. I could always smell a thief."

Smell yourself, Ted.

"And I knew I should call the police on this thief. I knew I should take that outfit away and find the real owner. But it was so beautiful, so perfect, that I gave the Indian stranger a thousand dollars and sent him on his way. And I kept the outfit."

Whoa, was Ted coming here to make a confession? And why had he chosen my grandmother's funeral for his confession?

"For years, I felt terrible. I'd look at that outfit hanging on the wall of my Montana cabin."

Mansion, Ted, it's a mansion. Go ahead; you can say it: MANSION!

"And then I decided to do some research. I hired an anthropologist, an expert, and he quickly pointed out that the outfit was obviously of Interior Salish origin. And after doing a little research, he discovered that the outfit was Spokane Indian, to be specific. And then, a few years ago, he visited your reservation undercover and learned that this stolen outfit once belonged to a woman named Grandmother Spirit."

We all gasped. This was a huge shock. I wondered if we were all part of some crazy reality show called *When Billionaires Pretend to be Human.* I looked around for the cameras.

"Well, ever since I learned who really owned this outfit, I've been torn. I always wanted to give it back. But I wanted to keep it, too. I couldn't sleep some nights because I was so torn up by it."

Yep, even billionaires have DARK NIGHTS OF THE SOUL.

"And, well, I finally couldn't take it anymore. I packed up the outfit and headed for your reservation, here, to hand-deliver the outfit back to Grandmother Spirit. And I get here only to discover that she's passed on to the next world. It's just devastating."

We were all completely silent. This was the weirdest thing

any of us had ever witnessed. And we're Indians, so trust me, we've seen some really weird stuff.

"But I have the outfit here," Ted said. He opened up his suitcase and pulled out the outfit and held it up. It was fifty pounds, so he struggled with it. Anybody would have struggled with it.

"So if any of Grandmother Spirit's children are here, I'd love to return her outfit to them."

My mother stood and walked up to Ted.

"I'm Grandmother Spirit's only daughter," she said.

My mother's voice had gotten all formal. Indians are good at that. We'll be talking and laughing and carrying on like normal, and then, BOOM, we get all serious and sacred and start talking like some English royalty.

"Dearest daughter," Ted said. "I hereby return your stolen goods. I hope you forgive me for returning it too late."

"Well, there's nothing to forgive, Ted," my mother said. "Grandmother Spirit wasn't a powwow dancer."

Ted's mouth dropped open.

"Excuse me," he said.

"My mother loved going to powwows. But she never danced. She never owned a dance outfit. This couldn't be hers."

Ted didn't say anything. He couldn't say anything.

"In fact, looking at the beads and design, this doesn't look Spokane at all. I don't recognize the work. Does anybody here recognize the beadwork?"

"No," everybody said.

"It looks more Sioux to me," my mother said. "Maybe Oglala. Maybe. I'm not an expert. Your anthropologist wasn't much of an expert, either. He got this *way* wrong."

We all just sat there in silence as Ted mulled that over.

Then he packed his outfit back into the suitcase, hurried over to his waiting car, and sped away.

For about two minutes, we all sat quiet. Who knew what to say? And then my mother started laughing.

And that set us all off.

Two thousands Indians laughed at the same time.

We kept laughing.

It was the most glorious noise I'd ever heard.

And I realized that, sure, Indians were drunk and sad and displaced and crazy and mean, but, dang, we knew how to laugh.

When it comes to death, we know that laughter and tears are pretty much the same thing.

And so, laughing and crying, we said good-bye to my grand-mother. And when we said good-bye to one grandmother, we said good-bye to all of them.

Each funeral was a funeral for all of us.

We lived and died together.

All of us laughed when they lowered my grandmother into the ground.

And all of us laughed when they covered her with dirt.

And all of us laughed as we walked and drove and rode our way back to our lonely, lonely houses.

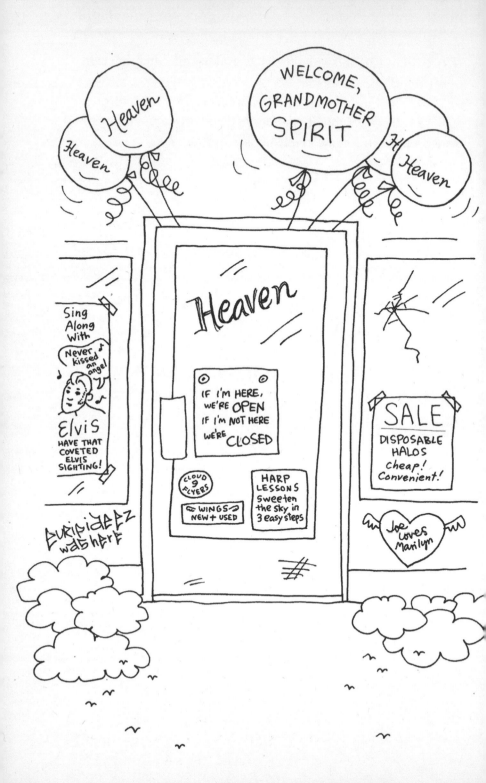

Valentine
Heart
✻

A few days after I gave Penelope a homemade Valentine (and she said she forgot it was Valentine's Day), my dad's best friend, Eugene, was shot in the face in the parking lot of a 7-Eleven in Spokane.

Way drunk, Eugene was shot and killed by one of his good friends, Bobby, who was too drunk to even remember pulling the trigger.

The police think Eugene and Bobby fought over the last drink in a bottle of wine:

When Bobby was sober enough to realize what he'd done, he could only call Eugene's name over and over, as if that would somehow bring him back.

A few weeks later, in jail, Bobby hung himself with a bedsheet.

We didn't even have enough time to forgive him.

He punished himself for his sins.

My father went on a legendary drinking binge.

My mother went to church every single day.

It was all booze and God, booze and God, booze and God.

We'd lost my grandmother and Eugene. How much loss were we supposed to endure?

I felt helpless and stupid.

I needed books.

I wanted books.

And I drew and drew and drew cartoons.

I was mad at God; I was mad at Jesus. They were mocking me, so I mocked them:

Jesus farteth and burpeth in harmony! MIRACULOUS!!
John 11:35am

I hoped I could find more cartoons that would help me. And I hoped I could find stories that would help me.

So I looked up the word "grief" in the dictionary.

I wanted to find out everything I could about grief. I wanted to know why my family had been given so much to grieve about.

And then I discovered the answer:

grief (grēef) n. When you feel so helpless and stupid that you think nothing will ever be right again, and your macaroni and cheese tastes like sawdust, and you can't even jerk off because it seems like too much trouble.
Webster's Dickshunary © 4ever

Okay, so it was Gordy who showed me a book written by the guy who knew the answer.

It was Euripides, this Greek writer from the fifth century BC.

A way-old dude.

In one of his plays, Medea says, "What greater grief than the loss of one's native land?"

I read that and thought, "Well, of course, man. We Indians have LOST EVERYTHING. We lost our native land, we lost our languages, we lost our songs and dances. We lost each other. We only know how to lose and be lost."

But it's more than that, too.

I mean, the thing is, Medea was so distraught by the world, and felt so betrayed, that she murdered her own kids.

She thought the world was that joyless.

And, after Eugene's funeral, I agreed with her. I could have easily killed myself, killed my mother and father, killed the birds, killed the trees, and killed the oxygen in the air.

More than anything, I wanted to kill God.

I was joyless.

I mean, I can't even tell you how I found the strength to get up every morning. And yet, every morning, I did get up and go to school.

Well, no, that's not exactly true.

I was so depressed that I thought about dropping out of Reardan.

I thought about going back to Wellpinit.

I blamed myself for all of the deaths.

I had cursed my family. I had left the tribe, and had broken something inside all of us, and I was now being punished for that.

No, my family was being punished.

I was healthy and alive.

Then, after my fifteenth or twentieth missed day of school, I sat in my social studies classroom with Mrs. Jeremy.

Mrs. Jeremy was an old bird who'd taught at Reardan for thirty-five years.

I slumped into her class and sat in the back of the room.

"Oh, class," she said. "We have a special guest today. It's Arnold Spirit. I didn't realize you still went to this school, Mr. Spirit."

The classroom was quiet. They all knew my family had been living inside a grief-storm. And had this teacher just mocked me for that?

"What did you just say?" I asked her.

"You really shouldn't be missing class this much," she said.

If I'd been stronger, I would have stood up to her. I would have called her names. I would have walked across the room and slapped her.

But I was too broken.

Instead, it was Gordy who defended me.

He stood with his textbook and dropped it.

Whomp!

He looked so strong. He looked like a warrior. He was protecting me like Rowdy used to protect me. Of course, Rowdy would have thrown the book at the teacher and then punched her.

Gordy showed a lot of courage in standing up to a teacher like that. And his courage inspired the others.

Penelope stood and dropped her textbook.

And then Roger stood and dropped his textbook.

Whomp!

Then the other basketball players did the same.

Whomp! Whomp! Whomp! Whomp!

And Mrs. Jeremy flinched each and every time, as if she'd been kicked in the crotch.

Whomp! Whomp! Whomp! Whomp!

Then all of my classmates walked out of the room.

A spontaneous demonstration.

Of course, I probably should have walked out with them.

It would have been more poetic. It would have made more sense. Or perhaps my friends should have realized that they shouldn't have left behind the FRICKING REASON FOR THEIR PROTEST!

And that thought just cracked me up.

It was like my friends had walked over the backs of baby seals in order to get to the beach where they could protest against the slaughter of baby seals.

Okay, so maybe it wasn't that bad.

But it was sure funny.

"What are you laughing at?" Mrs. Jeremy asked me.

"I used to think the world was broken down by tribes," I said. "By black and white. By Indian and white. But I know that isn't true. The world is only broken into two tribes: The people who are assholes and the people who are not."

I walked out of the classroom and felt like dancing and singing.

It all gave me hope. It gave me a little bit of joy.

And I kept trying to find the little pieces of joy in my life. That's the only way I managed to make it through all of that death and change. I made a list of the people who had given me the most joy in my life:

1. Rowdy
2. My mother
3. My father
4. My grandmother
5. Eugene
6. Coach
7. Roger
8. Gordy
9. Penelope, even if she only partially loves me

I made a list of the musicians who had played the most joyous music:

1. Patsy Cline, my mother's favorite
2. Hank Williams, my father's favorite
3. Jimi Hendrix, my grandmother's favorite
4. Guns N' Roses, my big sister's favorite
5. White Stripes, my favorite

I made a list of my favorite foods:

1. pizza
2. chocolate pudding
3. peanut butter and jelly sandwiches
4. banana cream pie
5. fried chicken
6. mac & cheese
7. hamburgers
8. french fries
9. grapes

I made a list of my favorite books:

1. The Grapes of Wrath
2. Catcher in the Rye
3. Fat Kid Rules the World
4. Tangerine
5. Feed
6. Catalyst
7. Invisible Man
8. Fools Crow
9. Jar of Fools

I made a list of my favorite basketball players:

1. Dwayne Wade
2. Shane Battier
3. Steve Nash
4. Ray Allen
5. Adam Morrison
6. Julius Erving
7. Kareem Abdul-Jabbar
8. George Gervin
9. Mugsy Bogues

I kept making list after list of the things that made me feel joy. And I kept drawing cartoons of the things that made me angry. I keep writing and rewriting, drawing and redrawing, and rethinking and revising and reediting. It became my grieving ceremony.

In Like a Lion

I'd never guessed I'd be a good basketball player.

I mean, I'd always loved ball, mostly because my father loved it so much, and because Rowdy loved it even more, but I figured I'd always be one of those players who sat on the bench and cheered his bigger, faster, more talented team-mates to victory and/or defeat.

But somehow or another, as the season went on, I became a freshman starter on a varsity basketball team. And, sure, all of my teammates were bigger and faster, but none of them could shoot like me.

I was the hired gunfighter.

Back on the rez, I was a decent player, I guess. A re-
bounder and a guy who could run up and down the floor without tripping. But something magical happened to me when I
went to Reardan.

Overnight, I became a good player.

I suppose it had something to do with confidence. I mean,
I'd always been the lowest Indian on the reservation totem
pole — I wasn't expected to be good so I wasn't. But in Rear-
dan, my coach and the other players wanted me to be good.
They needed me to be good. They expected me to be good.
And so I became good.

I wanted to live up to expectations.

I guess that's what it comes down to.

The power of expectations.

And as they expected more of me, I expected more of myself, and it just grew and grew until I was scoring twelve points
a game.

AS A FRESHMAN!

Coach was thinking I would be an all-state player in a few
years. He was thinking maybe I'd play some small-college ball.

It was crazy.

How often does a reservation Indian kid hear that?

How often do you hear the words "Indian" and "college"
in the same sentence? Especially in my family. Especially in
my tribe.

But don't think I'm getting stuck up or anything.

It's still absolutely scary to play ball, to compete, to try to win.

I throw up before every game.

Coach said he used to throw up before games.

"Kid," he said, "some people need to clear the pipes
before they can play. I used to be a yucker. You're a yucker
Ain't nothing wrong with being a yucker."

So I asked Dad if he used to be a yucker.

"What's a yucker?" he asked.

"Somebody who throws up before basketball games," I said.

"Why would you throw up?"

"Because I'm nervous."

"You mean, because you're scared?"

"Nervous, scared, same kind of things, aren't they?"

"Nervous means you want to play. Scared means you don't want to play."

All right, so Dad made it clear.

I was a nervous yucker in Reardan. Back in Wellpinit, I was a scared yucker.

Nobody else on my team was a yucker. Didn't matter one way or the other, I guess. We were just a good team, period.

After losing our first game to Wellpinit, we won twelve in a row. We just killed people, winning by double figures every time. We beat our archrivals, Davenport, by thirty-three.

Townspeople were starting to compare us to the great Reardan teams of the past. People were starting to compare some of our players to great players of the past.

Roger, our big man, was the new Joel Wetzel.

Jeff, our point guard, was the new Little Larry Soliday.

James, our small forward, was the new Keith Schulz.

But nobody talked about me that way. I guess it was hard to compare me to players from the past. I wasn't from the town, not originally, so I would always be an outsider.

And no matter how good I was, I would always be an Indian. And some folks just found it difficult to compare an Indian to a white guy. It wasn't racism, not exactly. It was, well, I don't know what it was.

I was something different, something new. I just hope

that, twenty years in the future, they'd be comparing some kid to me:

"Yeah, you see that kid shoot, he reminds me so much of Arnold Spirit."

Maybe that will happen. I don't know. Can an Indian have a legacy in a white town? And should a teenager be worried about his fricking legacy anyway?

Jeez, I must be an egomaniac.

Well, anyway, our record was 12 wins and 1 loss when we had our rematch with Wellpinit.

They came to our gym, so I wasn't going to get burned at the stake. In fact, my white fans were going to cheer for me like I was some kind of crusading warrior:

Jeez, I felt like one of those Indian scouts who led the U.S. Cavalry against other Indians.

But that was okay, I guess. I wanted to win. I wanted revenge. I wasn't playing for the fans. I wasn't playing for the white people. I was playing to beat Rowdy.

Yep, I wanted to embarrass my best friend.

He'd turned into a stud on his team. He was only a freshman, too, but he was averaging twenty-five points a game. I followed his progress in the sports section.

He'd led the Wellpinit Redskins to a 13–0 record. They were the number one–ranked small school in the state. Wellpinit had never been ranked that high. And it was all because of Rowdy. We were ranked number two, so our game was a big deal. Especially for a small-school battle.

And most especially because I was a Spokane Indian playing against his old friends (and enemies).

A local news crew came out to interview me before the game.

"So, Arnold, how does it feel to play against your former teammates?" the sports guy asked me.

"It's kind of weird," I said.

"How weird?"

"Really weird."

Yep, I was scintillating.

The sports guy stopped the interview.

"Listen," he said. "I know this is a difficult thing. You're young. But maybe you could get more specific about your feelings."

"My feelings?" I asked.

"Yeah, this is a major deal in your life, isn't it?"

Well, duh, yeah, of course it was a major deal. It was maybe the biggest thing in my life ever, but I wasn't about to share my feelings with the whole world. I wasn't going to start blubbering for the local sports guy like he was my priest or something.

I had some pride, you know?

I believed in my privacy.

It wasn't like I'd called the guy and offered up my story, you know?

And I was kind of suspicious that white people were really interested in seeing some Indians battle each other. I think it was sort of like watching dogfighting, you know?

It made me feel exposed and primitive.

"So, okay," the sports guy said. "Are you ready to try again?"

"Yeah."

"Okay, let's roll."

The camera guy started filming.

"So, Arnold," the sports guy said. "Back in December, you faced your old classmates, and fellow Spokane tribal members, in a basketball game back on the reservation, and you lost. They're now the number one–ranked team in the state and they're coming to your home gym. How does that make you feel?"

"Weird," I said.

"Cut, cut, cut, cut," the sports guy said. He was mad now.

"Arnold," he said. "Could you maybe think of a word besides weird?"

I thought for a bit.

"Hey," I said. "How about I say that it makes me feel like I've had to grow up really fast, too fast, and that I've come to realize that every single moment of my life is important. And that every choice I make is important. And that a basketball game, even a game between two small schools in the middle of nowhere, can be the difference between being happy and being miserable for the rest of my life."

"Wow," the sports guy said. "That's perfect. That's poetry. Let's go with that, okay?"

"Okay," I said.

"Okay, let's roll tape," the sports guy said again and put the microphone in my face.

"Arnold," he said. "Tonight you're going into battle against your former teammates and Spokane tribal members, the Wellpinit Redskins. They're the number one–ranked team in the state and they beat you pretty handily back in December. Some people think they're going to blow you out of the gym tonight. How does that make you feel?"

"Weird," I said.

"All right, all right, that's it," the sports guy said. "We're out of here."

"Did I say something wrong?" I asked.

"You are a little asshole," the sports guy said.

"Wow, are you allowed to say that to me?"

"I'm just telling the truth."

He had a point there. I was being a jerk.

"Listen, kid," the sports guy said. "We thought this was an important story. We thought this was a story about a kid striking out on his own, about a kid being courageous, and all you want to do is give us grief."

Wow.

He was making me feel bad.

"I'm sorry," I said. "I'm just a yucker."

"What?" the sports guy asked.

"I'm a nervous dude," I said. "I throw up before games. I think I'm just sort of, er, metaphorically throwing up on you. I'm sorry. The thing is, the best player on Wellpinit, Rowdy, he used to be my best friend. And now he hates me. He gave me a concussion that first game. And now I want to destroy him. I want to score thirty points on him. I want him to remember this game forever."

"Wow," the sports guy said. "You're pissed."

"Yeah, you want me to say that stuff on camera?"

"Are you sure you want to say that?"

"Yeah."

"All right, let's go for it."

They set up the camera again and the sports guy put the microphone back in my face.

"Arnold, you're facing off against the number one–ranked Wellpinit Redskins tonight and their all-star, Rowdy, who used to be your best friend back when you went to school on the reservation. They beat you guys pretty handily back in December, and they gave you a concussion. How does it feel to be playing them again?"

"I feel like this is the most important night of my life," I said. "I feel like I have something to prove to the people in Reardan, the people in Wellpinit, and to myself."

"And what do you think you have to prove?" the guy asked.

"I have to prove that I am stronger than everybody else. I have to prove that I will never give up. I will never quit playing hard. And I don't just mean in basketball. I'm never going to quit living life this hard, you know? I'm never going to surrender to anybody. Never, ever, ever."

"How bad do you want to win?"

"I never wanted anything more in my life."

"Good luck, Arnold, we'll be watching."

The gym was packed two hours before the game. Two thousand people yelling and cheering and stomping.

In the locker room, we all got ready in silence. But everybody, even Coach, came up to me and patted my head or shoulder, or bumped fists with me, or gave me a hug.

This was my game, this was my game.

I mean, I was still just the second guy off the bench, just the dude who provided instant offense. But it was all sort of warrior stuff, too.

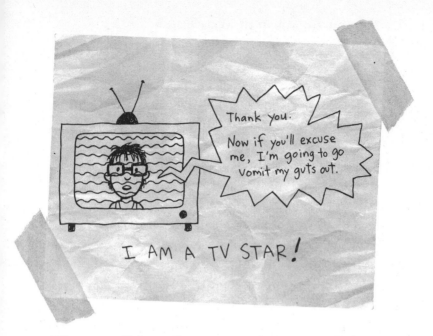

We were all boys desperate to be men, and this game would be a huge moment in our transition.

"Okay, everybody, let's go over the game plan," Coach said.

We all walked over to the chalkboard area and sat on folding chairs.

"Okay, guys," Coach said. "We know what these guys can do. They're averaging eighty points a game. They want to run and run and run. And when they're done running and gunning, they're going to run and gun some more."

Man, that wasn't much of a pep talk. It sounded like Coach was sure we were going to lose.

"And I have to be honest, guys," Coach said. "We can't beat these guys with our talent. We just aren't good enough. But I think we have bigger hearts. And I think we have a secret weapon."

I wondered if Coach had maybe hired some Mafia dude to take out Rowdy.

"We have Arnold Spirit," Coach said.

"Me?" I asked.

"Yes, you," Coach said. "You're starting tonight."

"Really?"

"Really. And you're going to guard Rowdy. The whole game. He's your man. You have to stop him. If you stop him, we win this game. It's the only way we're going to win this game."

Wow. I was absolutely stunned. Coach wanted me to guard Rowdy. Now, okay, I was a great shooter, but I wasn't a great defensive player. Not at all. There's no way I could stop Rowdy. I mean, if I had a baseball bat and bulldozer, maybe I could stop him. But without real weapons — without a pistol, a man-eating lion, and a vial of bubonic plague — I had zero chance of competing directly with Rowdy. If I guarded him, he was going to score seventy points.

"Coach," I said. "I'm really honored by this. But I don't think I can do it."

He walked over to me, kneeled, and pushed his forehead against mine. Our eyes were, like, an inch apart. I could smell the cigarettes and chocolate on his breath.

"You can do it," Coach said.

Oh, man, that sounded just like Eugene. He always shouted that during any game I ever played. It could be, like, a three-legged sack race, and Gene would be all drunk and happy in the stands and he'd be shouting out, "Junior, you can do it!"

Yeah, that Eugene, he was a positive dude even as an alcoholic who ended up getting shot in the face and killed.

Jeez, what a sucky life. I was about to play the biggest basketball game of my life and all I could think about was my dad's dead best friend.

So many ghosts.

"You can do it," Coach said again. He didn't shout it. He

whispered it. Like a prayer. And he kept whispering again. Until the prayer turned into a song. And then, for some magical reason, I believed in him.

Coach had become, like, the priest of basketball, and I was his follower. And I was going to follow him onto the court and shut down my best friend.

I hoped so.

"I can do it," I said to Coach, to my teammates, to the world.

"You can do it," Coach said.

"I can do it."

"You can do it."

"I can do it."

Do you understand how amazing it is to hear that from an adult? Do you know how amazing it is to hear that from anybody? It's one of the simplest sentences in the world, just four words, but they're the four hugest words in the world when they're put together.

You can do it.

I can do it.

Let's do it.

We all screamed like maniacs as we ran out of the locker room and onto the basketball court, where two thousand maniac fans were also screaming.

The Reardan band was rocking some Led Zeppelin.

As we ran through our warm-up layup drills, I looked up into the crowd to see if my dad was in his usual place, high up in the northwest corner. And there he was. I waved at him. He waved back.

Yep, my daddy was an undependable drunk. But he'd never missed any of my organized games, concerts, plays, or picnics. He may not have loved me perfectly, but he loved me as well as he could.

My mom was sitting in her usual place on the opposite side of the court from Dad.

Funny how they did that. Mom always said that Dad made her too nervous; Dad always said that Mom made him too nervous.

Penelope was yelling and screaming like crazy, too.

I waved at her; she blew me a kiss.

Great, now I was going to have to play the game with a boner.

Ha-ha, just kidding.

So we ran through layups and three-on-three weave drills and free throws and pick and rolls, and then the evil Wellpinit five came running out of the visitors' locker room.

Man, you never heard such booing. Our crowd was as loud as a jet.

They were just pitching the Wellpinit players some serious crap.

You want to know what it sounded like?

It sounded like this:

BOOOOOOOOOOOOOOOOOOOOOOOOOOOOO OOOOOOOOOOOOOOOOOOOOOOOOOOOOOOOO OOOOOOOOOOOOOOOOOOOOOOOOOOOOOOOO OOOOOOOOOOOOOOOOOOOOOOOOOOOOOOOO OOOOOOOOOOOOOOOOOOOOOO!

We couldn't even hear each other.

I worried that all of us were going to have permanent hearing damage.

I kept glancing over at Wellpinit as they ran their layup drills. And I noticed that Rowdy kept glancing over at us.

At me.

Rowdy and I pretended that we weren't looking at each other. But, man, oh, man, we were sending some serious hate signals across the gym.

I mean, you have to love somebody that much to also hate them that much, too.

Our captains, Roger and Jeff, ran out to the center circle to have the game talk with the refs.

Then our band played "The Star-Spangled Banner."

And then our five starters, including me, ran out to the center circle to go to battle against Wellpinit's five.

Rowdy smirked at me as I took my position next to him.

"Wow," he said. "You guys must be desperate if you're starting."

"I'm guarding you," I said.

"What?"

"I'm guarding you tonight."

"You can't stop me. I've been kicking your ass for fourteen years."

"Not tonight," I said. "Tonight's my night."

Rowdy just laughed.

The ref threw up the opening jump ball.

Our big guy, Roger, tipped it back toward our point guard, but Rowdy was quicker. He intercepted the pass and raced toward his basket. I ran right behind him. I knew that he wanted to dunk it. I knew that he wanted to send a message to us.

I knew he wanted to humiliate us on the opening play.

And for a second, I wondered if I should just intentionally foul him and prevent him from dunking. He'd get two free throws but those wouldn't be nearly as exciting as a dunk.

But, no, I couldn't do that. I couldn't foul him. That would be like giving up. So I just sped up and got ready to jump with Rowdy.

I knew he'd fly into the air about five feet from the hoop. I knew he'd jump about two feet higher than I could. So I needed to jump quicker.

And Rowdy rose into the air. And I rose with him.

AND THEN I ROSE ABOVE HIM!

Yep, if I believed in magic, in ghosts, then I think maybe I was rising on the shoulders of my dead grandmother and Eugene, my dad's best friend. Or maybe I was rising on my mother and father's hopes for me.

I don't know what happened.

But for once, and for the only time in my life, I jumped higher than Rowdy.

I rose above him as he tried to dunk it.

I TOOK THE BALL RIGHT OUT OF HIS HANDS!

Yep, we were, like, ten feet off the ground, but I was still able to reach out and steal the ball from Rowdy.

Even in midair, I could see the absolute shock on Rowdy's face. He couldn't believe I was flying with him.

He thought he was the only Indian Superman.

I came down with the ball, spun, and dribbled back toward our hoop. Rowdy, screaming with rage, was close behind me.

Our crowd was insanely loud.

They couldn't believe what I'd just done.

I mean, sure, that kind of thing happens in the NBA and in college and in the big high schools. But nobody jumped like that in a small school basketball gym. Nobody blocked a shot like that.

NOBODY TOOK A BALL OUT OF A GUY'S HANDS AS HE WAS JUST ABOUT TO DUNK!

But I wasn't done. Not by a long shot. I wanted to score. I'd taken the ball from Rowdy and now I wanted to score in his face. I wanted to absolutely demoralize him.

I raced for our hoop.

Rowdy was screaming behind me.

My teammates told me later that I was grinning like an idiot as I flew down the court.

I didn't know that.

I just knew I wanted to hit a jumper in Rowdy's face.

Well, I wanted to dunk on him. And I figured, with the crazy adrenaline coursing through my body, I might be able to jump over the rim again. But I think part of me knew that I'd never jump like that again. I only had that one epic jump in me.

I wasn't a dunker; I was a shooter.

So I screeched to a stop at the three-point line and head-faked. And Rowdy completely fell for it. He jumped high over me, wanting to block my shot, but I just waited for the sky to clear. As Rowdy hovered above me, as he floated away, he looked at me. I looked at him.

He knew he'd blown it. He knew he'd fallen for a little head-fake. He knew he could do nothing to stop my jumper.

He was sad, man.

Way sad.

So guess what I did?

I stuck my tongue out at him. Like I was Michael Jordan.

I mocked him.

And then I took my three-pointer and buried it. Just swished that sucker.

AND THE GYM EXPLODED!

People wept.

Really.

My dad hugged the white guy next to him. Didn't even know him. But hugged and kissed him like they were brothers, you know?

My mom fainted. Really. She just leaned over a bit, bumped against the white woman next to her, and was gone.

She woke up five seconds later.

People were up on their feet. They were high-fiving and hugging and dancing and singing.

The school band played a song. Well, the band members

were all confused and excited, so they played a song, sure, but each member of the band played a different song.

My coach was jumping up and down and spinning in circles.

My teammates were screaming my name.

Yep, all of that fuss and the score was only 3 to 0.

But, trust me, the game was over.

It only took, like, ten seconds to happen. But the game was already over. Really. It can happen that way. One play can determine the course of a game. One play can change your momentum forever.

We beat Wellpinit by forty points.

Absolutely destroyed them.

That three-pointer was the only shot I took that night. The only shot I made.

Yep, I only scored three points, my lowest point total of the season.

But Rowdy only scored four points.

I stopped him.

I held him to four points.

Only two baskets.

He scored on a layup in the first quarter when I tripped over my teammate's foot and fell.

And he scored in the fourth quarter, with only five seconds left in the game, when he stole the ball from me and raced down for a layup.

But I didn't even chase him down because we were ahead by forty-two points.

The buzzer sounded. The game was over. We had killed the Redskins. Yep, we had humiliated them.

We were dancing around the gym, laughing and screaming and chanting.

My teammates mobbed me. They lifted me up on their shoulders and carried me around the gym.

I looked for my mom, but she'd fainted again, so they'd taken her outside to get some fresh air.

I looked for my dad.

I thought he'd be cheering. But he wasn't. He wasn't even looking at me. He was all quiet-faced as he looked at something else.

So I looked at what he was looking at.

It was the Wellpinit Redskins, lined up at their end of the court, as they watched us celebrate our victory.

I whooped.

We had defeated the enemy! We had defeated the champions! We were David who'd thrown a stone into the brain of Goliath!

And then I realized something.

I realized that my team, the Reardan Indians, was Goliath.

I mean, jeez, all of the seniors on our team were going to college. All of the guys on our team had their own cars. All of the guys on our team had iPods and cell phones and PSPs and three pairs of blue jeans and ten shirts and mothers and fathers who went to church and had good jobs.

Okay, so maybe my white teammates had problems, serious problems, but none of their problems was life threatening.

But I looked over at the Wellpinit Redskins, at Rowdy.

I knew that two or three of those Indians might not have eaten breakfast that morning.

No food in the house.

I knew that seven or eight of those Indians lived with drunken mothers and fathers.

I knew that one of those Indians had a father who dealt crack and meth.

I knew two of those Indians had fathers in prison.

I knew that none of them was going to college. Not one of them.

And I knew that Rowdy's father was probably going to beat the crap out of him for losing this game.

I suddenly wanted to apologize to Rowdy, to all of the other Spokanes.

I was suddenly ashamed that I'd wanted so badly to take revenge on them.

I was suddenly ashamed of my anger, my rage, and my pain.

I jumped off my white teammates' shoulders and dashed into the locker room. I ran into the bathroom, into a toilet stall, and threw up.

And then I wept like a baby.

Coach and my teammates thought I was crying tears of happiness.

But I wasn't.

I was crying tears of shame.

I was crying because I had broken my best friend's heart.

But God has a way of making things even out, I guess.

Wellpinit never recovered from their loss to us. They only won a couple more games the rest of the season and didn't qualify for the playoffs.

However, we didn't lose another game in the regular season and were ranked number one in the state as we headed into the playoffs.

We played Almira Coulee-Hartline, this tiny farm-town team, and they beat us when this kid named Keith hit a crazy half-court shot at the buzzer. It was a big upset.

We all cried in the locker room for hours.

Coach cried, too.

I guess that's the only time that men and boys get to cry and not get punched in the face.

Rowdy and I Have a Long and Serious Discussion About Basketball ✵

A few days after basketball season ended, I e-mailed Rowdy and told him I was sorry that we beat them so bad and that their season went to hell after that.

"We'll kick your asses next year," Rowdy wrote back. "And you'll cry like the little faggot you are."

"I might be a faggot," I wrote back, "but I'm the faggot who beat you."

"Ha-ha," Rowdy wrote.

Now that might just sound like a series of homophobic

insults, but I think it was also a little bit friendly, and it was the first time that Rowdy had talked to me since I left the rez.

I was a happy faggot!

Because
Russian Guys
Are Not
Always
Geniuses
*

After my grandmother died, I felt like crawling into the coffin with her. After my dad's best friend got shot in the face, I wondered if I was destined to get shot in the face, too.

Considering how many young Spokanes have died in car wrecks, I'm pretty sure it's my destiny to die in a wreck, too.

Jeez, I've been to so many funerals in my short life.

I'm fourteen years old and I've been to forty-two funerals.

That's really the biggest difference between Indians and white people.

A few of my white classmates have been to a grandparent's funeral. And a few have lost an uncle or aunt. And one guy's brother died of leukemia when he was in third grade.

But there's nobody who has been to more than five funerals.

All my white friends can count their deaths on one hand.

I can count my fingers, toes, arms, legs, eyes, ears, nose, penis, butt cheeks, and nipples, and still not get close to my deaths.

And you know what the worst part is? The unhappy part? About 90 percent of the deaths have been because of alcohol.

Gordy gave me this book by a Russian dude named Tolstoy, who wrote: "Happy families are all alike; every unhappy family is unhappy in its own way." Well, I hate to argue with a Russian genius, but Tolstoy didn't know Indians. And he didn't know that all Indian families are unhappy for the same exact reason: the fricking booze.

Yep, so let me pour a drink for Tolstoy and let him think hard about the true definition of unhappy families.

So, okay, you're probably thinking I'm being extra bitter. And I would have to agree with you. I am being extra bitter. So let me tell you why.

Today, around nine a.m., as I sat in chemistry, there was a knock on the door, and Miss Warren, the guidance counselor, stepped into the room. Dr. Noble, the chemistry teacher, hates being interrupted. So he gave the old stink eye to Miss Warren.

"Can I help you, Miss Warren?" Dr. Noble asked. Except he made it sound like an insult.

"Yes," she said. "May I speak to Arnold in private?"

"Can this wait? We are going to have a quiz in a few moments."

"I need to speak with him now. Please."

"Fine. Arnold, please go with Miss Warren."

I gathered up my books and followed Miss Warren out into the hallway. I was a little worried. I wondered if I'd done something wrong. I couldn't think of anything I'd done that would merit punishment. But I was still worried. I didn't want to get into any kind of trouble.

"What's going on, Miss Warren?" I asked.

She suddenly started crying. Weeping. Just these big old whooping tears. I thought she was going to fall over on the floor and start screaming and kicking like a two-year-old.

"Jeez, Miss Warren, what is it? What's wrong?"

She hugged me hard. And I have to admit that it felt pretty dang good. Miss Warren was, like, fifty years old, but she was still pretty hot. She was all skinny and muscular because she jogged all the time. So I sort of, er, physically reacted to her hug.

And the thing is, Miss Warren was hugging me so tight that I was pretty sure she could feel my, er, physical reaction.

I was kind of proud, you know?

"Arnold, I'm sorry," she said. "But I just got a phone call from your mother. It's your sister. She's passed away."

"What do you mean?" I asked. I knew what she meant, but I wanted her to say something else. Anything else.

"Your sister is gone," Miss Warren said.

"I know she's gone," I said. "She lives in Montana now."

I knew I was being an idiot. But I figured if I kept being an idiot, if I didn't actually accept the truth, then the truth would become false.

"No," Miss Warren said. "Your sister, she's dead."

That was it. I couldn't fake my way around that. Dead is dead.

I was stunned. But I wasn't sad. The grief didn't hit me right away. No, I was mostly ashamed of my, er, physical reaction to the hug. Yep, I had a big erection when I learned of my sister's death.

How perverted is that? How inappropriately hormonal can one boy be?

"How did she die?" I asked.

"Your father is coming to get you," Miss Warren said. "He'll be here in a few minutes. You can wait in my office."

"How did she die?" I asked again.

"Your father is coming to get you," Miss Warren said again.

I knew then that she didn't want to tell me how my sister had died. I figured it must have been an awful death.

"Was she murdered?" I asked.

"Your father is coming."

Man, Miss Warren was a LAME counselor. She didn't know what to say to me. But then again, I couldn't really blame her. She'd never counseled a student whose sibling had just died.

"Was my sister murdered?" I asked.

"Please," Miss Warren said. "You need to talk to your father."

She looked so sad that I let it go. Well, I mostly let it go. I certainly didn't want to wait in her office. The guidance office was filled with self-help books and inspirational posters and SAT test books and college brochures and scholarship applications, and I knew that none of that, absolutely none of it, meant shit.

I knew I'd probably tear her office apart if I had to wait there.

"Miss Warren," I said, "I want to wait outside."

"But it's snowing," she said.

"Well, that would make it perfect, then, wouldn't it?" I said.

It was a rhetorical question, meaning there wasn't supposed to be an answer, right? But poor Miss Warren, she answered my rhetorical question.

"No, I don't think it's a good idea to wait in the snow," she said. "You're very vulnerable right now."

VULNERABLE! She told me I was vulnerable. My big sister was dead. Of course I was vulnerable. I was a reservation Indian attending an all-white school and my sister had just died some horrible death. I was the most vulnerable kid in the United States. Miss Warren was obviously trying to win the Captain Obvious Award.

"I'm waiting outside," I said.

"I'll wait with you," she said.

"Kiss my ass," I said and ran.

Miss Warren tried to run after me. But she was wearing heels and she was crying and she was absolutely freaked out by my reaction to the bad news. By my cursing. She was nice. Too nice to deal with death. So she just ran a few feet before she stopped and slumped against the wall.

I ran by my locker, grabbed my coat, and headed outside. There was maybe a foot of snow on the ground already. It was going to be a big storm. I suddenly worried that my father was going to wreck his car on the icy roads.

Oh, man, wouldn't that just be perfect?

Yep, how Indian would that be?

Imagine the stories I could tell.

"Yeah, when I was a kid, just after I learned that my big sister died, I also found out that my father died in a car wreck on the way to pick me up from school."

So I was absolutely terrified as I waited.

I prayed to God that my father would come driving up in his old car.

"Please, God, please don't kill my daddy. Please, God,

please don't kill my daddy. Please, God, please don't kill my daddy."

Ten, fifteen, twenty, thirty minutes went by. I was freezing. My hands and feet were big blocks of ice. Snot ran down my face. My ears were burning cold.

"Oh, Daddy, please, oh, Daddy, please, oh, Daddy, please."

Oh, man, I was absolutely convinced that my father was dead, too. It had been too long. He'd driven his car off a cliff and had drowned in the Spokane River. Or he'd lost control, slid across the centerline, and spun right into the path of a logging truck.

"Daddy, Daddy, Daddy, Daddy."

And just when I thought I'd start screaming, and run around like a crazy man, my father drove up.

I started laughing. I was so relieved, so happy, that I LAUGHED. And I couldn't stop laughing.

I ran down the hill, jumped into the car, and hugged my dad. I laughed and laughed and laughed and laughed.

"Junior," he said. "What's wrong with you?"

"You're alive!" I shouted. "You're alive!"

"But your sister —," he said.

"I know, I know," I said. "She's dead. But you're alive. You're still alive."

I laughed and laughed. I couldn't stop laughing. I felt like I might die of laughing.

I couldn't figure out why I was laughing. But I kept laughing as my dad drove out of Reardan and headed through the storm back to the reservation.

And then, finally, as we crossed the reservation border, I stopped laughing.

"How did she die?" I asked.

"There was a big party at her house, her trailer in Montana —," he said.

Yep, my sister and her husband lived in some old silver trailer that was more like a TV dinner tray than a home.

"They had a big party —," my father said.

OF COURSE THEY HAD A BIG PARTY! OF COURSE THEY WERE DRUNK! THEY'RE INDIANS!

"They had a big party," my father said. "And your sister and her husband passed out in the back bedroom. And somebody tried to cook some soup on a hot plate. And they forgot about it and left. And a curtain drifted in on the wind and caught the hot plate, and the trailer burned down quick."

I swear to you that I could hear my sister screaming.

"The police say your sister never even woke up," my father said. "She was way too drunk."

My dad was trying to comfort me. But it's not too comforting to learn that your sister was TOO FREAKING DRUNK to feel any pain when she BURNED TO DEATH!

And for some reason, that thought made me laugh even harder. I was laughing so hard that I threw up a little bit in my mouth. I spit out a little piece of cantaloupe. Which was weird, because I don't like cantaloupe. I've hated cantaloupe since I was a little kid. I couldn't remember the last time I'd eaten the evil fruit.

And then I remembered that my sister had always loved cantaloupe.

Ain't that weird?

It was so freaky that I laughed even harder than I'd already been laughing. I started pounding the dashboard and stomping on the floor.

I was going absolutely insane with laughter.

My dad didn't say a word. He just stared straight ahead and drove home. I laughed the whole way. Well, I laughed until we were about halfway home, and then I fell asleep.

Snap, just like that.

Things had gotten so intense, so painful, that my body just checked out. Yep, my mind and soul and heart had a quick meeting and voted to shut down for a few repairs.

And guess what? I dreamed about cantaloupe!

Well, I dreamed about a school picnic I went to way back when I was seven years old. There were hot dogs and hamburgers and soda pop and potato chips and watermelon and cantaloupe.

I ate, like, seven pieces of cantaloupe.

My hands and face were way sticky and sweet.

I'd eaten so much cantaloupe that I'd turned into a cantaloupe.

Well, I finished my lunch and I ran around the playground, laughing and screaming, when I felt this tickle on my cheek. I reached up to scratch my face and squished the wasp that had been sucking sugar off my cheek.

Have you ever been stung in the face? Well, I have, and that's why I hate cantaloupe.

So, I woke up from this dream, this nightmare, just as my dad drove the car up to our house.

"We're here," he said.

"My sister is dead," I said.

"Yes."

"I was hoping I dreamed that," I said.

"Me, too."

"I dreamed about that time I got stung by the wasp," I said.

"I remember that," Dad said. "We had to take you to the hospital."

"I thought I was going to die."

"We were scared, too."

My dad started to cry. Not big tears. Just little ones. He breathed deep and tried to stop them. I guess he wanted to be strong in front of his son. But it didn't work. He kept crying.

I didn't cry.

I reached out, wiped the tears off my father's face, and tasted them.

Salty.

"I love you," he said.

Wow.

He hardly ever said that to me.

"I love you, too," I said.

I never said that to him.

We walked into the house.

My mom was curled into a ball on the couch. There were, like, twenty-five or thirty cousins there, eating all of our food.

Somebody dies and people eat your food. Funny how that works.

"Mom," I said.

"Oh, Junior," she said and pulled me onto the couch with her.

"I'm sorry, Mom. I'm so sorry."

"Don't leave me," she said. "Don't ever leave me."

She was freaking out. But who could blame her? She'd lost her mother and her daughter in just a few months. Who ever recovers from a thing like that? Who ever gets better? I knew that my mother was now broken and that she'd always be broken.

"Don't you ever drink," my mother said to me. She slapped me. Once, twice, three times. She slapped me HARD. "Promise me you'll never drink."

"Okay, okay, I promise," I said. I couldn't believe it. My sister killed herself with booze and I was the one getting slapped.

Where was Leo Tolstoy when I needed him? I kept wishing he'd show up so my mother could slap him instead.

Well, my mother quit slapping me, thank God, but she held on to me for hours. Held on to me like I was a baby. And she kept crying. So many tears. My clothes and hair were soaked with her tears.

It was, like, my mother had given me a grief shower, you know?

Like she'd baptized me with her pain.

Of course, it was way too weird to watch. So all of my cousins left. My dad went in his bedroom.

It was just my mother and me. Just her tears and me.

But I didn't cry. I just hugged my mother back and wanted all of it to be over. I wanted to fall asleep again and dream about killer wasps. Yeah, I figured any nightmare would be better than my reality.

And then it was over.

My mother fell asleep and let me go.

I stood and walked into the kitchen. I was way hungry but my cousins had eaten most of our food. So all I had for dinner were saltine crackers and water.

Like I was in jail.

Man.

Two days later, we buried my sister in the Catholic graveyard down near the powwow ground.

I barely remember the wake. I barely remember the funeral service. I barely remember the burial.

I was in this weird fog.

No.

It was more like I was in this small room, the smallest room in the world. I could reach out and touch the walls, which were made out of greasy glass. I could see shadows but I couldn't see details, you know?

And I was cold.

Just freezing.

Like there was a snowstorm blowing inside of my chest.

But all of that fog and greasy glass and snow disappeared when they lowered my sister's coffin into the grave. And let me tell you, it had taken them forever to dig that grave in the frozen ground. As the coffin settled into the dirt, it made this noise, almost like a breath, you know?

Like a sigh.

Like the coffin was settling down for a long, long nap, for a forever nap.

That was it.

I had to get out of there.

I turned and ran out of the graveyard and into the woods across the road. I planned on running deep into the woods. So deep that I'd never be found.

But guess what?

I ran full-speed into Rowdy and sent us both sprawling.

Yep, Rowdy had been hiding in the woods while he watched the burial.

Wow.

Rowdy sat up. I sat up, too.

We sat there together.

Rowdy was crying. His face was shiny with tears.

"Rowdy," I said. "You're crying."

"I ain't crying," he said. "You're crying."

I touched my face. It was dry. No tears yet.

"I can't remember how to cry," I said.

That made Rowdy sort of choke. He gasped a little. And more tears rolled down his face.

"You're crying," I said.

"No, I'm not."

"It's okay; I miss my sister, too. I love her."

"I said I'm not crying."

"It's okay."

I reached out and touched Rowdy's shoulder. Big mistake. He punched me. Well, he almost punched me. He threw a punch but he MISSED!

ROWDY MISSED A PUNCH!

His fist went sailing over my head.

"Wow," I said. "You missed."

"I missed on purpose."

"No, you didn't. You missed because your eyes are FILLED WITH TEARS!"

That made me laugh.

Yep, I started laughing like a crazy man again.

I rolled around on the cold, frozen ground and laughed and laughed and laughed.

I didn't want to laugh. I wanted to stop laughing. I wanted to grab Rowdy and hang on to him.

He was my best friend and I needed him.

But I couldn't stop laughing.

I looked at Rowdy and he was crying hard now.

He thought I was laughing at him.

Normally, Rowdy would have absolutely murdered anybody who dared to laugh at him. But this was not a normal day.

"It's all your fault," he said.

"What's my fault?" I asked.

"Your sister is dead because you left us. You killed her."

That made me stop laughing. I suddenly felt like I might never laugh again.

Rowdy was right.

I had killed my sister.

Well, I didn't kill her.

But she only got married so quickly and left the rez because I had left the rez first. She was only living in Montana in a cheap trailer house because I had gone to school in Reardan. She had burned to death because I had decided that I wanted to spend my life with white people.

It was all my fault.

"I hate you!" Rowdy screamed. "I hate you! I hate you!"

And then he jumped up and ran away.

Rowdy ran!

He'd never run away from anything or anybody. But now he was running.

I watched him disappear into the woods.

I wondered if I'd ever see him again.

The next morning, I went to school. I didn't know what else to do. I didn't want to sit at home all day and talk to a million cousins. I knew my mother would be cooking food for everybody and that my father would be hiding out in his bedroom again.

I knew everybody would tell stories about Mary.

And the whole time, I'd be thinking, "Yeah, but have you ever heard the story about how I killed my sister when I left the rez?"

And the whole time, everybody would be drinking booze and getting drunk and stupid and sad and mean. Yeah, doesn't that make sense? How do we honor the drunken death of a young married couple?

HEY, LET'S GET DRUNK!

Okay, listen, I'm not a cruel bastard, okay? I know that people were very sad. I knew that my sister's death made everybody remember all the deaths in their life. I know that death is never added to death; it multiplies. But still, I couldn't stay and watch all of those people get drunk. I couldn't do it. If you'd given me a room full of sober Indians, crying and laughing and telling stories about my sister, then I would have gladly stayed and joined them in the ceremony.

But everybody was drunk.

Everybody was unhappy.

And they were drunk and unhappy in the same exact way.

So I fled my house and went to school. I walked through the snow for a few miles until a white BIA worker picked me up and delivered me to the front door.

I walked inside, into the crowded hallways, and all sorts of boys and girls, and teachers, came up and hugged me and slapped my shoulder and gave me little punches in the belly.

They were worried for me. They wanted to help me with my pain.

I was important to them.

I mattered.

Wow.

All of these white kids and teachers, who were so suspicious of me when I first arrived, had learned to care about me. Maybe some of them even loved me. And I'd been so suspicious of them. And now I care about a lot of them. And loved a few of them.

Penelope came up to me last.

She was WEEPING. Snot ran down her face and it was still sort of sexy.

"I'm so sorry about your sister," she said.

I didn't know what to say to her. What do you say to people when they ask you how it feels to lose everything? When every planet in your solar system has exploded?

My Final Freshman Year Report Card

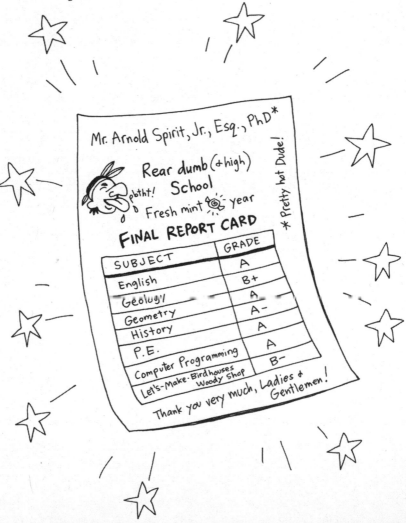

Mr. Arnold Spirit, Jr., Esq., PhD*

Rear dumb (& high) School

pbtht!

Fresh mint year

FINAL REPORT CARD

* Pretty hot Dude!

SUBJECT	GRADE
	A
English	B+
Geology	A
Geometry	A-
History	A
P.E.	A
Computer Programming	
Let's-Make-Birdhouses Woody Shop	B-

Thank you very much, Ladies & Gentlemen!

Remembering

✳

Today my mother, father, and I went to the cemetery and cleaned graves.

We took care of Grandmother Spirit, Eugene, and Mary.

Mom had packed a picnic and Dad had brought his saxophone, so we made a whole day of it.

We Indians know how to celebrate with our dead.

And I felt okay.

My mother and father held hands and kissed each other.

"You can't make out in a graveyard," I said.

"Love and death," my father said. "It's all love and death."

"You're crazy," I said.

"I'm crazy about you," he said.

And he hugged me.

And he hugged my mother.

And she had tears in her eyes.

And she held my face in her hands.

"Junior," she said. "I'm so proud of you."

· That was the best thing she could have said.

In the middle of a crazy and drunk life, you have to hang on to the good and sober moments tightly.

I was happy. But I still missed my sister, and no amount of love and trust was going to make that better.

I love her. I will always love her.

I mean, she was amazing. It was courageous of her to leave the basement and move to Montana. She went searching for her dreams, and she didn't find them, but she made the attempt.

And I was making the attempt, too. And maybe it would kill me, too, but I knew that staying on the rez would have killed me, too.

It all made me cry for my sister. It made me cry for myself.

But I was crying for my tribe, too. I was crying because I knew five or ten or fifteen more Spokanes would die during the next year, and that most of them would die because of booze.

I cried because so many of my fellow tribal members were slowly killing themselves and I wanted them to live. I wanted them to get strong and get sober and get the hell off the rez.

It's a weird thing.

Reservations were meant to be prisons, you know? Indians were supposed to move onto reservations and die. We were supposed to disappear.

But somehow or another, Indians have forgotten that reservations were meant to be death camps.

I wept because I was the only one who was brave and crazy enough to leave the rez. I was the only one with enough arrogance.

I wept and wept and wept because I knew that I was never going to drink and because I was never going to kill myself and because I was going to have a better life out in the white world.

I realized that I might be a lonely Indian boy, but I was not alone in my loneliness. There were millions of other Americans who had left their birthplaces in search of a dream.

I realized that, sure, I was a Spokane Indian. I belonged to that tribe. But I also belonged to the tribe of American immigrants. And to the tribe of basketball players. And to the tribe of bookworms.

And the tribe of cartoonists.

And the tribe of chronic masturbators.

And the tribe of teenage boys.

And the tribe of small-town kids.

And the tribe of Pacific Northwesterners.

And the tribe of tortilla chips-and-salsa lovers.

And the tribe of poverty.

And the tribe of funeral-goers.

And the tribe of beloved sons.

And the tribe of boys who really missed their best friends.

It was a huge realization.

And that's when I knew that I was going to be okay.

But it also reminded me of the people who were not going to be okay.

It made me think of Rowdy.

I missed him so much.

I wanted to find him and hug him and beg him to forgive me for leaving.

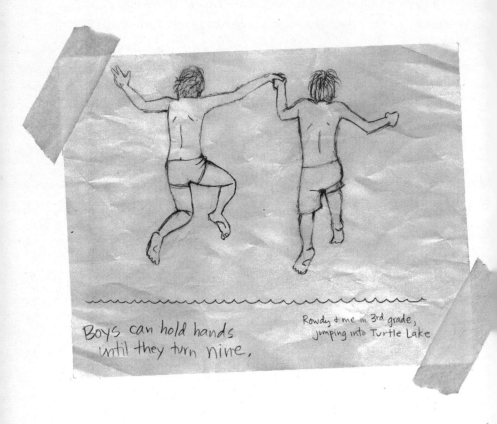

Boys can hold hands
until they turn nine.

Rowdy & me in 3rd grade,
jumping into Turtle Lake

Talking
About
Turtles
✳

The reservation is beautiful.

I mean it.

Take a look.

There are pine trees everywhere. Thousands of ponderosa pine trees. Millions. I guess maybe you can take pine trees for granted. They're just pine trees. But they're tall and thin and green and brown and big.

Some of the pines are ninety feet tall and more than three hundred years old.

Older than the United States.

Some of them were alive when Abraham Lincoln was president.

Some of them were alive when George Washington was president.

Some of them were alive when Benjamin Franklin was born. ·

I'm talking old.

I've probably climbed, like, one hundred different trees in my lifetime. There are twelve in my backyard. Another fifty or sixty in the small stand of woods across the field. And another twenty or thirty around our little town. And a few way out in the deep woods.

And that tall monster that sits beside the highway to West End, past Turtle Lake.

That one is way over one hundred feet tall. It might be one hundred and fifty feet tall. You could build a house using just the wood from that tree.

When we were little, like ten years old, Rowdy and I climbed that sucker.

It was probably stupid. Yeah, okay, it was stupid. It's not like we were lumberjacks or anything. It's not like we used anything except our hands, feet, and dumb luck.

But we weren't afraid of falling that day.

Other days, yeah, I'm terrified of falling. No matter how old I get, I think I'm always going to be scared of falling. But I wasn't scared of gravity on that day. Heck, gravity didn't even *exist*.

It was July. Crazy hot and dry. It hadn't rained in, like, sixty days. Drought hot. Scorpion hot. Vultures flying circles in the sky hot.

Mostly Rowdy and I just sat in my basement room, which was maybe five degrees cooler than the rest of the house, and read books and watched TV and played video games.

Mostly Rowdy and I just sat still and dreamed about air-conditioning.

"When I get rich and famous," Rowdy said, "I'm going to have a house that has an air conditioner in every room."

"Sears has those big air conditioners that can cool a whole house," I said.

"Just one machine?" Rowdy asked.

"Yeah, you put it outside and you connect it through the air vents and stuff."

"Wow, how much does that cost?"

"Like, a few thousand bucks, I think."

"I'll never have that much money."

"You will when you play in the NBA."

"Yeah, but I'll probably have to play pro basketball in, like, Sweden or Norway or Russia or something, and I won't need air-conditioning. I'll probably live in, like, an igloo and own reindeer or something."

"You're going to play for Seattle, man."

"Yeah, right."

Rowdy didn't believe in himself. Not much. So I tried to pump him up.

"You're the toughest kid on the rez," I said.

"I know," he said.

"You're the fastest, the strongest."

"And the most handsome, too."

"If I had a dog with a face like yours, I'd shave its ass and teach it to walk backwards."

"I once had a zit that looked like you. Then I popped it. And then it looked even more like you."

"This one time, I ate, like, three hot dogs and a bowl of clam chowder, and then I got diarrhea all over the floor, and it looked like you."

"And then you ate it," Rowdy said.

We laughed ourselves silly. We laughed ourselves sweaty.

"Don't make me laugh," I said. "It's too hot to laugh."

"It's too hot to sit in this house. Let's go swimming."

"Where?"

"Turtle Lake."

"Okay," I said.

But I was scared of Turtle Lake. It was a small body of water, maybe only a mile around. Maybe less. But it was deep, crazy deep. Nobody has ever been to the bottom. I'm not a very good swimmer; so I was always afraid I'd sink and drown, and they'd never, ever find my body.

One year, these scientists came with a mini-submarine and tried to find the bottom, but the lake was so silty and muddy that they couldn't see. And the nearby uranium mine made their radar/sonar machines go nuts, so they couldn't see that way, either, so they never made it to the bottom.

The lake is round. Perfectly round. So the scientists said it was probably an ancient and dormant volcano crater.

Yeah, a volcano on the rez!

The lake was so deep because the volcano crater and tunnels and lava chutes and all that plumbing went all the way down to the center of the earth. That lake was, like, *forever* deep.

There were all sorts of myths and legends surrounding the lake. I mean, we're Indians, and we like to make up shit about lakes, you know?

Some people said the lake is named Turtle because it's round and green like a turtle's shell.

Some people said it's named Turtle because it used to be filled with regular turtles.

Some people said it's named Turtle because it used to be home to this giant snapping turtle that ate Indians.

A Jurassic turtle. A Steven Spielberg turtle. A King Kong versus the Giant Reservation Turtle turtle.

I didn't exactly believe in the giant turtle myth. I was too old and smart for that. But I'm still an Indian, and we like to be scared. I don't know what it is about us. But we love ghosts. We love monsters.

But I was really scared of this other story about Turtle Lake.

My dad told me the story.

When he was a kid he watched a horse drown in Turtle Lake and disappear.

"Some of the others say it was a giant turtle that grabbed the horse," Dad said. "But they're lying. They were just being silly. That horse was just stupid. It was so stupid we named it Stupid Horse."

Well, Stupid Horse sank into the endless depths of Turtle Lake and everybody figured that was the end of that story.

But a few weeks later, Stupid Horse's body washed up on the shores of Benjamin Lake, ten miles away from Turtle Lake.

"Everybody just figured some joker had found the body and moved it," Dad said. "To scare people."

People laughed at the practical joke. Then a bunch of guys threw the dead horse into the back of a truck, drove it to the dump, and burned it.

Simple story, right?

No, it doesn't end there.

"Well, a few weeks after they burned the body, a bunch of kids were swimming in Turtle Lake when it caught fire."

YES, THE WHOLE LAKE CAUGHT ON FIRE!

The kids were swimming close to the dock. Because the lake was so deep, most kids swam close to shore. And the fire started out in the middle of the lake, so the kids were able to safely climb out of the water before it all went up like a big bowl of gasoline.

"It burned for a few hours," Dad said. "Burned hot and fast. And then it went out. Just like that. People stayed away for a few days then went to take a look at the damage, you know? And guess what they found? Stupid Horse washed up on shore again."

Despite being burned at the dump, and burned again in the lake of fire, Stupid Horse was untouched. Well, the horse was still dead, of course, but it was unburned. Nobody went near the horse after that. They just let it rot. But it took a long time — too long. For weeks, the dead body just lay there. Didn't go bad or anything. Didn't stink. The bugs and animals stayed away. Only after a few weeks did Stupid Horse finally let go. His skin and flesh melted away. The maggots and coyotes ate their fill. Then the horse was just bones.

"Let me tell you," Dad said. "That was just about the scariest thing I've ever seen. That horse skeleton lying there. It was freaky."

After a few more weeks, the skeleton collapsed into a pile of bones. And the water and the wind dragged them away.

It was a freaky story!

"Nobody swam in Turtle Lake for ten, eleven years," Dad said.

Me, I don't think anybody should be swimming in there now. But people forget. They forget good things and they forget bad things. They forget that lakes can catch on fire. They forget that dead horses can magically vanish and reappear.

I mean, jeez, we Indians are just weird.

So, anyway, on that hot summer day, Rowdy and I walked the five miles from my house to Turtle Lake. All the way, I thought about fire and horses, but I wasn't going to tell Rowdy about that. He would've just called me a wuss or a pussy. He would've just said it was kid stuff. He would've just said it was a hot day that needed a cold lake.

As we walked, I saw that monster pine tree ahead of us.

It was so tall and green and beautiful. It was the only reservation skyscraper, you know?

"I love that tree," I said.

"That's because you're a tree fag," Rowdy said.

"I'm not a tree fag," I said.

"Then how come you like to stick your dick inside knot-holes?"

"I stick my dick in the girl trees," I said.

Rowdy laughed his ha-ha, hee-hee avalanche laugh.

I loved to make him laugh. I was the only one who knew how to make him laugh.

"Hey," he said. "You know what we should do?"

I hated when Rowdy asked that particular question. It meant we were about to do something dangerous.

"What should we do?" I asked.

"We should climb that monster."

"That tree?"

"No, we should climb your big head," he said. "Of course, I'm talking about that tree. The biggest tree on the rez."

It wasn't really open to debate. I had to climb the tree. Rowdy knew I had to climb the tree with him. I couldn't back down. That wasn't how our friendship worked.

"We're going to die," I said.

"Probably," Rowdy said.

So we walked over to the tree and looked up. It was way tall. I got dizzy.

"You first," Rowdy said.

I spit on my hands, rubbed them together, and reached up for the first branch. I pulled myself up to the next branch. And then the next and the next and the next. Rowdy followed me.

Branch by branch, Rowdy and I climbed toward the top of the tree, to the bottom of the sky.

Near the top, the branches got thinner and thinner. I wondered if they'd support our weight. I kept expecting one of them to snap and send me plummeting to my death.

But it didn't happen.

The branches would not break.

Rowdy and I climbed and climbed and climbed. We made it to the top. Well, almost to the top. Even Rowdy was too scared to step on the thinnest branches. So we made it within ten feet of the top. Not the summit. But close enough to call it the summit.

We clung tightly to the tree as it swung in the breeze.

I was scared, sure, terrified . . . but it was also fun, you know?

We were more than one hundred feet in the air. From our vantage point, we could see for miles. We could see from one end of the reservation to the other. We could see our entire world. And our entire world, at that moment, was green and golden and perfect.

"Wow," I said.

"It's pretty," Rowdy said. "I've never seen anything so pretty."

It was the only time I'd ever heard him talk like that.

We stayed in the top of the tree for an hour or two. We didn't want to leave. I thought maybe we'd stay up there and die. I thought maybe two hundred years later, scientists would find two boy skeletons stuck in the top of that tree.

But Rowdy broke the spell.

He farted. A greasy one. A greasy, smelly one that sounded like it was half solid.

"Jeez," I said. "I think you just killed the tree."

We laughed.

And then we climbed down.

I don't know if anybody else has ever climbed that tree. I look at it now, years later, and I can't believe we did it.

And I can't believe I survived my first year at Reardan.

After the last day of school ended, I didn't do much. It was summer. I wasn't supposed to do anything. I mostly sat in my room and read comics.

I missed my white friends and white teachers and my translucent semi-girlfriend.

Ah, Penelope!

I hoped she was thinking about me.

I'd already written her three love letters. I hoped she'd write me back.

Gordy wanted to come to the rez and stay with us for a week or two. How crazy was that?

And Roger, heading to Eastern Washington University on a football scholarship, had willed his basketball uniform to me.

"You're going to be a star," he said.

I felt hopeful and silly about the future.

And then, yesterday, I was sitting in the living room, watching some nature show about honeybees, when there was a knock on the door.

"Come in!" I shouted.

And Rowdy walked inside.

"Wow," I said.

"Yeah," he said.

We'd always been such scintillating conversationalists.

"What are you doing here?" I asked.

"I'm bored," he said.

"The last time I saw you, you tried to punch me," I said.

"I missed."

"I thought you were going to break my nose."

"I wanted to break your nose."

"You know," I said. "It's probably not the best thing in the world to do, punching a hydro in the skull."

"Ah, shoot," he said. "I couldn't give you any more brain

damage than you already got. And besides, didn't I give you one concussion already?"

"Yep, and three stitches in my forehead."

"Hey, man, I had nothing to do with those stitches. I only do concussions."

I laughed.

He laughed.

"I thought you hated me," I said.

"I do," he said. "But I'm bored."

"So what?"

"So you want to maybe shoot some hoops?"

For a second, I thought about saying no. I thought about telling him to bite my ass. I thought about making him apologize. But I couldn't. He was never going to change.

"Let's go," I said.

We walked over to the courts behind the high school.

Two old hoops with chain nets.

We just shot lazy jumpers for a few minutes. We didn't talk. Didn't need to talk. We were basketball twins.

Of course, Rowdy got hot, hit fifteen or twenty in a row, and I rebounded and kept passing the ball to him.

Then I got hot, hit twenty-one in a row, and Rowdy rebounded for me.

"You want to go one-on-one?" Rowdy asked.

"Yeah."

"You've never beaten me one-on-one," he said. "You pussy."

"Yeah, that's going to change."

"Not today," he said.

"Maybe not today," I said. "But someday."

"Your ball," he said and passed it to me.

I spun the rock in my hands.

"Where you going to school next year?" I asked.

"Where do you think, dumb-ass? Right here, where I've always been."

"You could come to Reardan with me."

"You already asked me that once."

"Yeah, but I asked you a long time ago. Before everything happened. Before we knew stuff. So I'm asking you again. Come to Reardan with me."

Rowdy breathed deeply. For a second, I thought he was going to cry. Really. I expected him to cry. But he didn't.

"You know, I was reading this book," he said.

"Wow, you were reading a book!" I said, mock-surprised.

"Eat me," he said.

We laughed.

"So, anyway," he said. "I was reading this book about old-time Indians, about how we used to be nomadic."

"Yeah," I said.

"So I looked up nomadic in the dictionary, and it means people who move around, who keep moving, in search of food and water and grazing land."

"That sounds about right."

"Well, the thing is, I don't think Indians are nomadic anymore. Most Indians, anyway."

"No, we're not," I said.

"I'm not nomadic," Rowdy said. "Hardly anybody on this rez is nomadic. Except for you. You're the nomadic one."

"Whatever."

"No, I'm serious. I always knew you were going to leave. I always knew you were going to leave us behind and travel the world. I had this dream about you a few months ago. You were standing on the Great Wall of China. You looked happy. And I was happy for you."

Rowdy didn't cry. But I did.

"You're an old-time nomad," Rowdy said. "You're going to keep moving all over the world in search of food and water and grazing land. That's pretty cool."

I could barely talk.

"Thank you," I said.

"Yeah," Rowdy said. "Just make sure you send me postcards, you asshole."

"From everywhere," I said.

I would always love Rowdy. And I would always miss him, too. Just as I would always love and miss my grandmother, my big sister, and Eugene.

Just as I would always love and miss my reservation and my tribe.

I hoped and prayed that they would someday forgive me for leaving them.

I hoped and prayed that I would someday forgive myself for leaving them.

"Ah, man," Rowdy said. "Stop crying."

"Will we still know each other when we're old men?" I asked.

"Who knows anything?" Rowdy asked.

Then he threw me the ball.

"Now quit your blubbering," he said. "And play ball."

I wiped my tears away, dribbled once, twice, and pulled up for a jumper.

Rowdy and I played one-on-one for hours. We played until dark. We played until the streetlights lit up the court. We played until the bats swooped down at our heads. We played until the moon was huge and golden and perfect in the dark sky.

We didn't keep score.

The Absolutely True Diary of a Part-Time Indian

10th
ANNIVERSARY
EDITION
BONUS
CONTENT

Contents

A Note from Sherman Alexie

Okay, so you just finished reading *The Absolutely True Diary of a Part-Time Indian*. Maybe it's the first time you've read it. Maybe it's the hundredth. In any case, thank you for paying attention to my story. Thanks to all of you who've paid attention to this book over the last ten years. This novel is a decade old! That seems impossible, right? Time is a trickster.

So I guess this Tenth Anniversary Edition of *True Diary* is like a birthday celebration. And this afterword is like a birthday song. That's cool. But it should be something bigger than that, as well. I think I should use this afterword to tell you something new about *True Diary* and some of the people and places and events and ideas that inspired me to write it.

Okay? So here we go.

The hero of this book is Arnold Spirit Jr. The other hero of this book is Rowdy.

I didn't write Rowdy as a hero. I never intended him to be heroic. But he was not supposed to be a villain, either. He was meant to be a messy and contradictory human: bitter and funny, loyal and angry, loving and vindictive. He was Arnold's best friend, but he was also going to become Arnold's worst enemy.

And yes, there would be reconciliation, but it would be complicated and competitive. Is there such a thing as antagonistic forgiveness? I don't know if that happens in real life, but I tried to write it into this novel.

After all, if you turn back to the first page and read this book again, then you will discover that Rowdy never really stops being a jerk. How did this jerk become so lovable?

I had never thought of Rowdy as being lovable. I never even gave him a last name. At least, I don't think I gave him a last name. I haven't read *True Diary* in a while. I am sure that I have forgotten certain details. There's also another thing: I had surgery to remove a benign brain tumor in December 2015, and that successful operation also removed some of my long-term memories.

In any case, what kind of character doesn't get a last name? What kind of character is given a violent name? A violent dude! How could I have predicted that a violent character would become the subject of fascination and affection?

"Is Rowdy real?" readers have asked me thousands of times in the decade since *True Diary* was published. It is often the first question in any classroom, bookstore, or university lecture hall. Reporters ask me if Rowdy is based on a real person. I have received hundreds of letters from fans begging me to confirm that Rowdy is real.

And the answer is "Yes, Rowdy is real."

Rowdy is indeed based on my childhood best friend on the Spokane Indian Reservation. But I completely disguised the connection between the fictional character and the real person. How thorough was that disguise? Rowdy's real name is Randy.

Randy J. Peone.

So, okay, "Rowdy" and "Randy" are almost synonyms. But Rowdy and Randy differ in significant ways. Unlike Rowdy, Randy is not a single child. He has, like, eighteen thousand brothers and sisters, all of them ridiculously attractive. Unlike Rowdy's angry father, Randy has a mother and father who are loving and supportive. For many years, Randy has lived in a house only five minutes away from his parents. Unlike Rowdy, Randy liked school. He studied science in college and has worked for our tribal fish hatchery for as long as I can remember.

However, our dear Randy has always had a mean temper, like Rowdy. He has always liked to fight, physically and verbally. He has struggled with depression and anger issues. Sometimes he drinks too much. Sometimes he is cruel to his family and friends. So, yeah, Rowdy and Randy also have a lot in common.

Don't worry. Randy read this book before it was published, and he signed a release letter that stated he was cool with his fictional avatar.

"Junior," he said to me during a phone call, "the book is good. But I didn't punch you in the face when you left Wellpinit."

"Yes, you did," I said.

"Nope," he said.

We argued about that point for a while. We, as they say, agreed to disagree. And then, a few months later, on a publicity visit in Miami, I dreamed of the day when Randy had punched me and sent me to my new school, to Reardan, with a fresh black eye. Except in my dream, a different kid slugged me.

I woke from that dream and realized Randy wasn't the one who'd punched me. It was a different Indian boy, one of my damned bullies. I thought about calling up Randy to apologize. But then I remembered that he had definitely punched me in the nose after a Little League baseball game. Well, I had punched him first, but that was only because he'd been picking on me, just like one of my eternal bullies. Randy was supposed to be my best friend. He was supposed to be my protector. So I punched him in the face for betraying me. And then he punched me back. But he punched me *harder*. I think he broke my nose. I never went to the doctor. I let it heal on its own. And my nose has been a little flatter ever since.

So, okay, Randy did not punch me when I left him for Reardan. But he had slugged me one year earlier. I think the fictional and real punches had very similar *emotional content*.

And I think Randy would probably agree with me. Or maybe he would argue with me. Maybe he'd be right to argue. After all, as I think about our Little League two-punch fight, I think I might have overreacted to Randy's teasing. But, hey, I had been chronically bullied. I did have the grade school PTSD of a battered kid. So maybe I had been reflexively conditioned to meet any aggression, however mild, moderate, or wild, with my own aggression.

I don't know for sure.

I will never know for sure.

Because on December 8, 2016, Randy J. Peone died in a car wreck on a narrow two-lane highway north of Spokane, Washington. He was not intoxicated. The roads were clean and clear. The sky was blue. Visibility was good. Rowdy was alone in his car, so nobody knows for sure why he drifted across the center line and struck a car in the opposite lane. One of his brothers suspects that Randy might have been distracted by his phone. He liked to text and drive. The other drivers were hospitalized for their injuries but survived. There were also three children in the other cars, but they were not injured.

Randy sustained massive head and internal injuries and died that night without ever regaining consciousness.

He had not been wearing his seat belt.

In 2016, what kind of foolish, impulsive, and risk-embracing idiot refuses to wear his seat belt?

Come on, Randy! What were you thinking?

I did not receive the news about Randy's death until the next morning. I had been writing and, as usual, ignoring my cell phone. But then my sister called my home landline at the same moment Randy's sister-in-law sent an urgent e-mail.

I immediately called Randy's sister-in-law, and she told me the terrible news. I had not spoken to Randy in many years. I had not seen him in an even longer period. But I was instantly transported back in time, and I wept and wailed like a twelve-year-old boy whose best friend had just died.

I was Sherman Alexie Jr., mourning the sudden death of Randy Peone. And I was Arnold Spirit Jr., mourning the sudden death of Rowdy. My real and fictional lives blended in torturous ways.

"Oh my God," I said to his sister-in-law. "I loved him. I loved him. I loved him."

Five days later, I stood beside his open coffin in the funeral home. I kissed Randy on the forehead. I put my hand on his chest. Randy had always been short, only five four as an adult, but he'd always been built like a wolverine. Thick and muscular. But in his coffin, Randy looked skinny. In my memory, Randy was a vibrant teenager, a fullback, point guard, and fastball pitcher. And now, in the present, he was a forty-nine-year-old man — killed in a car wreck — who'd dealt with the typical and atypical health problems of a middle-aged Native American. Age had turned him smaller and darker. He'd always been handsome — a blue-eyed Indian — and he was still handsome, dressed in a white shirt and Indian-design vest, as he rested in his coffin.

I turned away from Randy so I could address the gathered mourners. So I could memorialize him.

I saw dozens of Indians I had known for my whole life, and I saw their children, who I didn't know at all. I'd been in kindergarten with some of those Indians. One of those Indians had been my favorite babysitter. I saw Randy's brothers and sisters, and his mother and father, and his children.

I saw my brothers and sisters sitting in the back row of seats.

And then I spoke.

I hadn't written anything down.

I hadn't prepared.

I spoke directly from the heart, partly as the reservation boy I used to be, the skinny and unknown Indian kid named Junior. And partly as the urban Indian named Sherman, who'd somehow become an unskinny and famous writer.

I felt unreal. Like I had been transported into one of my own books. But the characters in books live forever. And real people die.

I closed my eyes, inhaled, exhaled, opened my eyes, and spoke. And this, to the best of my compromised memory, is what I said:

When I heard about Randy's death, I instantly thought about the movie *Stand by Me*, based on the novella *The Body*, by Stephen King. I thought about the end of that movie, when we learn that Chris Chambers, played as a kid by River Phoenix, became a lawyer. And we also learn that he was stabbed to death while trying to break up a fight in a fast-food restaurant. A tragic, unpredictable death. I have seen that movie a hundred times, at least, but I still cry every time. And I really cry when Gordie Lachance, played by Richard Dreyfuss as an adult, types those amazing, amazing words: *I never had any friends later on like the ones I had when I was twelve. Jesus, does anyone?*

So I thought about being twelve years old in Wellpinit, and I thought about Randy, who was my best friend back then. I thought about his tragic, unpredictable death. And I realized that I've never again had a friend like him. I have never really had a friend as important to me, as necessary, as Randy.

You all remember me when I was twelve. And when I was younger. Skinny and sickly and smart and smart-ass and wearing those government glasses that weighed about thirty pounds.

A lot of kids bullied me. Some of you in this room, some of you bullied me. You know who you are. I certainly remember you.

Ha! Yeah, it's good to laugh. It's good to tease. We're Indians. So we know that teasing can be an act of love.

But you old bullies shouldn't worry too much about how mean you used to be. I forgive you. A little bit. But I really wonder how many of you remember hurting me? And maybe I hurt some of you, too, and I don't remember it. If I ever hurt you, then I am sorry. We were all young and foolish. We were reservation Indian kids, and that was difficult for all of us.

I like to joke and tell people that I'm not one of those Indians who believe in magic, but I believe in interpreting coincidence exactly the way I want to.

I don't know if it was a coincidence that Randy came to Wellpinit in sixth grade. He lived only fifteen miles away from my house. But he went to school in Springdale. And I had never met him. The world was a different place back then. It was bigger and smaller at the same time. You could belong to the same tribe, and live on the same reservation only fifteen miles apart, and be the same age, but you could still be strangers to each other.

So I didn't know Randy on his first day of school in Wellpinit. He was small. But he looked mean and tough. Like he was a fighter. You all remember how much we used to punch one another? Boys fighting boys. Girls fighting girls. Girls fighting boys. And almost everybody beating me up. It seemed like that, anyway. I know a lot of you were good kids. I know a lot of you were just as scared and hurting as I was. But you don't notice that stuff when you're a kid. Your own life feels so huge that it's hard to see anybody else's life.

So Randy walks into the classroom. He struts on his little Peone legs. He looks like he will fight anybody. Like he will fight the weather. And I think, "Oh, great, somebody else to bully me."

So I avoid him all day. I even hide in the speech therapy room so I don't have to go outside at recess and maybe get punched.

But it turns out that Randy was getting bullied, instead of the other way around. And Stevie was the worst. You all remember how mean Stevie could be? He went after Randy, the new kid, the new Indian. So Stevie pushes and pushes and pushes Randy, and then Randy pushes back and says, "We're fighting after school."

So, after school, everybody runs up to the old playground to watch the fight. But I run home because I know somebody will get all pumped up by the first fight and will get me into the second fight. I can see the old playground from my front window, so I sit there and watch it all happen.

Everybody stands in a circle around Stevie and Randy.

And I can see Stevie talking. I can't hear what he's saying, but I know he's probably telling Randy to throw the first punch. Remember how we did that? We'd always tell the other person to throw the first punch. Why did we do that? If you're going to fight, then you should want to throw the first punch, right? Anyway, Stevie says, "Throw the first punch," and Randy doesn't even hesitate. He says, "Okay," and punches Stevie in the face and knocks him out. Knocks him unconscious. What twelve-year-old kid has knockout power like that? Only Randy.

At first, I was excited because Randy had just defeated the meanest bully. And then I got depressed because that meant Randy was meaner than the meanest bully. There was *proof*. And that meant I was in big trouble.

So I was terrified to go to school the next day. But I did. And everybody was talking about Randy's punch, even the high schoolers. I sat at my desk and shook with fear. And then Randy walked into the classroom and sat beside me.

He said, "What's your name?"

I wanted to run. I knew he'd make fun of my speech impediments — of my lisp and stutter. I knew he'd make fun of my big hydrocephalic head and my government glasses. I knew he'd make fun of how easily I cried, and then he would make fun of my crying.

"Hey," he said. "What's your name?"

"Junior," I said.

"I'm Randy J. Peone," he said, and smiled.

And then it happened. We all know about falling in love at first sight. Most of us have probably fallen in love at first sight with somebody. Hopefully, with the person you're married to right now. Love at first sight is always romantic, right? But have you ever heard about people becoming best friends at first sight? Have you ever heard of two Indian boys becoming instant best friends? Becoming best friends the first time they ever talk to each other? After they've only said maybe ten words to each other?

Well, that happened to Randy and me. I don't know how to explain it. But Randy and I were suddenly best friends. We never talked about it. We never acknowledged it. We just *knew*. Both of us *knew*. And that's just how it was always going to be.

And let me tell you, after Randy became my best friend, I

didn't get bullied all that much anymore. Randy became my bodyguard.

He was the one who made me a good basketball player. Remember, I was the sick kid. The weak kid. The kid with seizures. But Randy got me on the basketball court and assumed that I would be good. He absolutely believed that I was good. He had so much confidence in himself that it made me confident in myself.

And so, because of Randy, I was a good basketball player *overnight*. It was magical. And he and I led our sixth-grade team to an undefeated season and the VFW championship. But we didn't even really need the other players. I think Randy and I could have won that league playing two-on-five.

In practice one day, Randy and I played our seven teammates in a short game and beat them 21–6. Some of those teammates are here. I bet you're still mad about losing to a two-man team.

Ha!

Yeah, it's good to laugh at funerals. It's good to be happy and sad at the same time.

But you all know Randy was a great athlete. I couldn't believe how many trophies he'd won. The first time I went to his house, I had to pick up and study every trophy. He was great at everything. Football, baseball, track, wrestling, boxing. I didn't even play any of those sports. And he was better at basketball. At first.

And I hate to say this at Randy's funeral, with him right there in his coffin, unable to talk trash back to me, but I eventually ended up being a better basketball player than he was. I think he knew it, too. But he never admitted it. Randy would never admit to something like that. We played against each other only twice. In eighth grade. When I was at Reardan and he was still at Wellpinit.

Randy won that first game in Wellpinit, when Billy Shawn and Marty Andrews were the refs. They weren't even real refs. They were high school kids. And they fouled me out in the third quarter.

But back in Reardan, when we had real refs, we swamped Wellpinit. We won the game by thirty points. And I guarded Randy and held him to two points. It would have been zero points, but my own teammate tripped me on the last play of the game, and Randy broke free and got a layup. They'd lost the game by thirty points, but Randy still talked trash at me because he'd scored that last hoop.

He talked trash about that for years.

"Remember that time when I faked you out and you fell down and I drove for that layup?" he'd say.

"I got tripped," I'd say. "And that was your only basket of the game."

"I don't remember that," he'd say.

"And we beat you by thirty."

"Don't remember that, either."

Randy and I never stopped being competitive. But basketball wasn't the best thing that we shared.

You see, Randy was the first person who really listened to me. I'd stay the night at his house. He'd sleep on the bottom bunk, and I'd be on the top bunk. And I would do most of the talking. Wherever I've gone in my life, I've usually done most of the talking. Talk, talk, talk, that's me. So Randy and I would stay awake all night, and I would talk about the girls I loved.

Some of you girls are in this room. You're women now, and I'm still a little bit in love with some of you.

Ha!

No, I'm not going to say who.

But, hey, none of you loved me back. Not as a boyfriend. So my heart was always broken. I would talk about you, the girls I loved who did not love me back, and I would cry. I would cry *hard*. Randy never made fun of me for crying. He would listen and listen and listen, and he would tell me that you girls didn't deserve my love. He'd tell me the love of my life was somewhere else in the world and that she and I would find each other. Randy was only twelve years old, and he was saying that smart and romantic stuff.

But he would also give me advice. He'd challenge me. This one time, he said, "Junior, you fall in love too easy."

And, oh man, he was right about that.

The thing is, whether we were talking about basketball or girls or school or anything else, Randy was the first person who always, always, always made me feel loved. Made me feel appreciated. Made me feel *understood*.

And yeah, in the meantime he was fighting and arguing with almost everybody else. With kids and adults.

But he was always good to me.

And so I started to believe that I was good. I started to believe I was great. More than that, I started to believe that a little Indian boy like me could compete against white people.

Do you remember how it felt to be so Indian and so poor and so powerless? And it felt like you would lose to white people? That you'd *always* lose to white people?

Well, Randy didn't believe that. And he wouldn't let me believe it, either. He wouldn't let me believe I was inferior to white people. Or to other Indians.

Randy had so much faith in me. It was amazing.

And it feels weird to say this. It sounds hurtful, maybe. But I think Randy's faith in me gave me the faith to leave the reservation school and transfer to Reardan.

I think about my older son. He was really sick when he was born, and he needed a lot of speech therapy and physical therapy as he grew older. For a few years, he did hippotherapy.

I know that sounds like he rode hippos. Ha!

But actually he rode horses as a way to build up his muscles and his confidence.

And one day as he was riding, the horse trainer said that my son was "borrowing the strength of the horse until he could find his own."

So I'm not calling Randy a horse here, but I think that I borrowed his strength. I think I absolutely needed to borrow his strength in Wellpinit, on the reservation, until I found my own strength off the reservation.

And you guys mostly know what happened in high school. I became a basketball star in Reardan. Eventually, Randy left Wellpinit a couple years after I did. He went back to school in Springdale and became a basketball star, too. We never played each other in high school, though, because his teams were terrible and my teams were good.

Ha! I had to talk trash one more time.

You see, at Reardan, I played with white boys who were good at basketball. At Springdale, Randy played with white boys who weren't good.

Ha!

Randy and I became friendly again over the years, mostly because of basketball. In all-star high school tournaments. And then in all-Indian tournaments after high school.

I remember when I hit two clutch free throws to beat his team in an all-Indian tournament in Springdale. He was so mad at losing but so happy that I'd hit the game winner. Laughing, he picked me up, slung me over his shoulder, and ran me around the gym. Then he carried me outside, through the gym doors, and threw me into a snowbank.

I saw him only once or twice when we were in college. One night, during my last semester at Washington State University, I boozed my way to the reservation, to Wellpinit. I was depressed. And struggling with my bipolar mental illness. I didn't know I was bipolar. I wouldn't be officially diagnosed for twenty more years. I was getting drunk every weekend. I was falling apart.

I don't remember how Randy and I ended up together that night. But we drove drunk around the reservation for hours and crashed five or six or eight parties.

It's all a blur.

At some point, in somebody's house on the rez, I stood and started reciting my poems from memory. In those early days, I could recite all of my poems by heart.

So there I was, drunkenly reciting my poems about life on the reservation while standing in a house on my reservation. I would publish my first book, *The Business of Fancydancing*, eighteen months later. And my future wife, the love of my life, would attend my first reading of that book in Spokane a few weeks after that.

I also got sober in March 2001 and have been sober ever since.

But I was almost blind drunk on that blurred night on my rez. And I recited poetry! That was so goofy and arrogant! Maybe some of you were there. I remember that some Indians tried to heckle me. But Randy, ever my protector, silenced them with a mean stare. And then he, ever the listener, sat in front of me, a one-person audience. I don't know how long I recited poetry, but I do know that Randy paid attention.

And I remember that I wept that night and told Randy how afraid I was of being trapped again. I was afraid of becoming a reservation drunk. I told him I wanted to become a professional poet, a real writer, and there was no way it would ever happen. I told Randy that I was doomed to fail.

But Randy stood and grabbed my shoulders. He was nearly as drunk as I was. He was young and strong, so it hurt when he grabbed me. He wasn't my best friend anymore. We'd stopped being best friends when I left the reservation school. When I left Wellpinit.

Let me be real honest here. When I left Wellpinit, I also left my best friend. And that's like a betrayal, right? No, it isn't *like* a betrayal. It is betrayal. In leaving, I betrayed my best friend. In leaving, I betrayed my tribe. But sometimes you have to do that. I have lived an amazing life. I think I have changed the whole world for the better. At least a little bit. And I know my books, my stories, have helped a lot of people. A lot of other Indians. And none of that would've happened if I hadn't left Wellpinit. Great things have happened to me because I left. But it has also caused me so much pain. And I know it caused all of you pain, too. I know some of you are still mad at me for leaving. That's okay. I understand.

But you have to understand that I didn't leave because I wanted to hurt any of you. I left because I wanted to save myself. I am happy I left the reservation. My life has been magical. But I know I gave up so much. I know I lost so much beauty when I left.

But, hey, most of you don't know this. All of it almost fell apart. *I* almost fell apart. I ended up drunk on the reservation that night, reciting my poetry, and I was ready to give up. I had given up.

But Randy, my handsome, blue-eyed Indian, stared hard at me, and he said, "Junior, those poems are amazing. You're going to be famous."

"No," I said. "That's not me."

"You're going to travel the whole world reading your poems," he said.

"But what about you?" I asked.

"I'm always going to be here," he said. "And you'll always be somewhere else. Somewhere bigger."

"That's not fair," I said. "It's not fair to you."

"You just have to send me postcards," he said. "You have to be a postcard Indian. You have to send me postcards from everywhere in the world."

Well, I don't think I ever sent one postcard to Randy J. Peone. But I wrote a novel about him. And I've discovered that millions of people love the fictional version of Randy.

Randy, I don't know if you knew how important Rowdy has become to people. And I never told you how important you have always been to me. We didn't talk about things like that. We didn't talk about us.

But I do know some good things.

I am a storyteller because you listened to me.

I am alive because you lived.

And, like I said earlier, I don't believe in magic. I don't believe in God, either. But I thank God anyway for you. I thank God you stepped into that sixth-grade classroom and asked me my name.

Dear Randy J. Peone, dear Rowdy, I love you so much. And I will miss you forever.

Personal Photos from Sherman

Arnold, my big brother; my younger sisters, twins Kim and Arlene; and me piling on my father, Sherman Alexie Sr. It was taken by my mother in 1971 in our nineteenth-century house on the Spokane Indian Reservation. At this point, we lived in our one-bedroom house with our big sister, Mary; my father's grandmother Lizzie and his great-uncle Stubby; and five adult cousins, Johnny, Tinker, Bill, Eugene, and Sam.

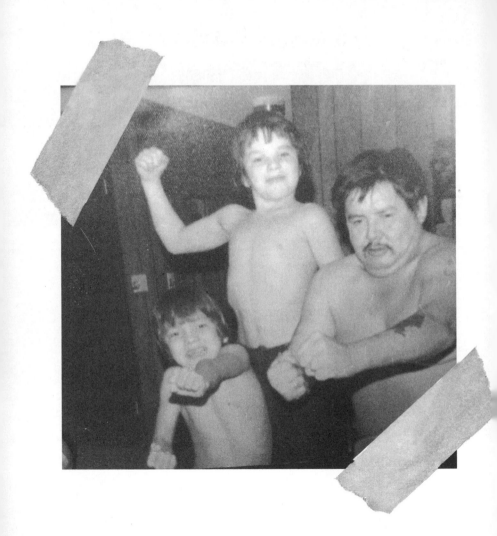

Me, my big brother, and my father pretending to be Bruce Lee. It was taken by my mother in 1975 in our house constructed by the Department of Housing and Urban Development. My father had just returned from a ten-day drinking binge, and we were happy to have him home.

This is me, six feet two inches and 145 pounds, hitting a jumper against Harrington High School during my senior year. We were an undersized and underdog team that year but won our district playoffs by defeating Ritzville and Davenport, who finished second and third in the Class B state tournament. We lost our two games in the state tourney, and I still have nightmares about those losses.

Beardan High School Annual, 1985

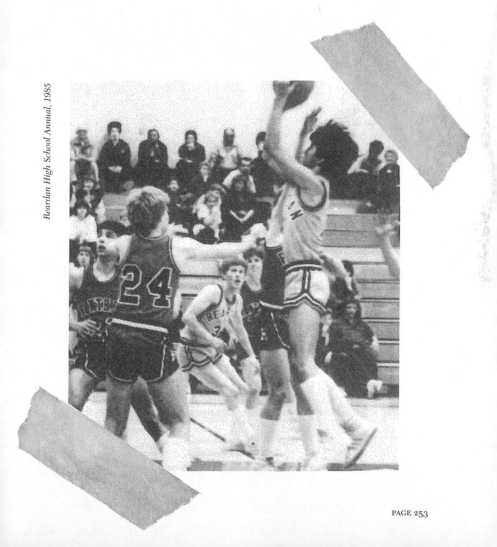

The late Randy J. Peone, my childhood best friend and the inspiration for Rowdy. I will miss him forever.

Springdale High School Annual, 1985

This is the day of my graduation from Reardan High School
with my best friends, Rick Williams, Tom Beitey, Doug Fiess,
and Gordon Tyus. We all graduated from high school and
college with academic honors. You could say I was best
friends with four white boy geniuses. Tom died in 1991, but
the other three are doing well. I don't have much contact
with them, but I remember them with love and respect.

A **never-before-seen**, unedited excerpt from an unfinished and unpublished sequel to *The Absolutely True Diary of a Part-Time Indian*, from **Rowdy's point of view.**

Rowdy, Rowdy, Rowdy

by Sherman Alexie

SEPTEMBER 5

Everybody loves a meteor, but hardly anybody cares about a meteorite.

SEPTEMBER 6

A meteor is called a shooting star, an amazing name, but it's only space junk set afire as it enters our atmosphere and burns to nothing. During meteor showers, people gather in large numbers and "ooh" and "aah" and talk about God's fireworks and the last time they saw something so beautiful and the world is an amazing place and I love you and let's be happy forever and blah, blah, frigging blah. And the nightly news sends a reporter into the foothills to let viewers know when and where to see the prettiest part of a meteor shower. And people, actually believing in the news for the first time, put on their shoes and coats and rush out to watch.

So, yeah, big butt cheers for the meteor.

As for the meteorite? That's a piece of space junk that made it through the flames and survived the impact with the earth. It can be a piece of dust or a house-sized boulder. But big or small, there are no television reports and no celebrations and no big crowds to celebrate a meteorite. Imagine walking up to a crowd circling a baseball-sized meteorite.

"Hey, what's going on?" you'd ask the friendliest-looking dude.

"We're celebrating," he'd say, and point with his lips at the space baseball.

"You're celebrating a rock?"

"It's a meteorite."

"You mean a shooting star?"

"Sort of. This is a shooting star that survived. It's amazing."

"It's a rock."

"It's a survivor."

"It's a small rock."

"It was burning at three thousand degrees Fahrenheit when it passed through the earth's atmosphere."

"Okay, it's a hot small rock."

"It's a testament to the awesome power of the universe."

"It looks like a baseball."

SEPTEMBER 7

So, yeah, the question is: Do you want to be a meteor or a meteorite?

Or maybe the question is: Do you want to be the Spokane Indian guy who shot off the reservation like a star and made white people fall in love with his brilliance? Or do you want to be the Spokane Indian who survived the other guy's flames and sits alone and small and uncelebrated on the rez among all the other space baseballs?

Or maybe the question should be: Do you want to be Arnold Spirit Jr., the little asshole who was good at drawing cartoons, playing basketball, doing math, writing English papers, making people laugh, and every other thing but somehow always convinced people that he lived a difficult life despite the fact that he had two loving parents who let him leave our shitty Indian school and go to the awesome white school on the reservation border? Or do you want to be me, Rowdy Polatkin, who is not quite as smart or funny or talented as Arnold Spirit Jr. and is trapped on the reservation and gets beaten by his drunken father once or twice a month while his drunken mother cries in the corner, too afraid to do anything because she'll get beaten even worse?

Pretty goddamn easy choice, don't you think?

SEPTEMBER 8

And yeah, I know I just used three curse words in my last entry. And in case you don't remember them, let me repeat them in order of appearance: asshole, shitty, goddamn.

And I know some of you (teachers and preachers) are offended and scandalized, but I also know that most of you cuss when you stub your toe on a table or run over a dog with your car or grab an electric fence that you didn't know was electrified.

So imagine that you are stubbing your toe, running over dogs, and getting fence-shocked every *asshole* minute of every *shitty* day of your *goddamn* life, and then you'll realize that the only words that can accurately tell the story are the curse words.

And if you still don't understand me or agree with my writing advice, then feel free to use the cut-and-paste button in your head and change "asshole" to "awful," "shitty" to "terrible," and "goddamn" to "damn."

SEPTEMBER 9

Okay, so I went off on a detour yesterday. That's okay. Real life is a series of detours, shortcuts, and dead ends. And if you want to tell a good story, then it better be about real life.

But in order to make a good story even better, you should also come back and repeat the main point. You should make sure that people "get it." So let me return to my meteor-versus-meteorite argument.

To remind you, the meteor is Arnold Spirit Jr., and I, Rowdy Polatkin, am the meteorite.

Arnold used to be my best friend, but now he is my worst enemy.

There is nobody you can hate as much as somebody you used to love.

A Letter from an Educator

Dear Readers,

As a high school English teacher, I find that one of my most critical challenges is selecting reading material that both captivates and instructs my students. I'm always reminding myself that most of my students are not future English teachers; they won't all adore parsing literature because it's a fun puzzle, or simply love reading for reading's sake. Many of them view English class as an exercise in endurance—and for some, survival. Assigned books are so often the lima beans of the high school experience, to be suffered or dodged.

Sometimes, however, a novel comes along that flaunts the label "selected text." It instructs students while captivating them.

They cannot put it down. They come to class each morning ready to talk about the "crazy stuff" that happened in the book last night. They read too fast and finish before the due date. Sherman Alexie's *The Absolutely True Diary of a Part-Time Indian* is this book, the unicorn of assigned reading: a book every kid wants to read.

Why? I asked a few students who recently read *The Diary*, as we call it.

"It's relatable to kids and stuff they've gone through."

"It's funny, so it keeps you reading. Even the sad parts are funny."

"It gives us a chance to talk about stereotypes."

"It was so good — this is the only book I've ever read."

That final comment is a reprise of a line I hear every year, sometimes more than once per year. You may wonder, how do students make it to high school without ever having read a book? Despite the best intentions and efforts of all these students' elementary, middle, and high school teachers, librarians, parents, and others, these students have never found a love for reading. They've not felt the connection to a character that compelled them to reach for that book again. They haven't found a story line that warrants giving up outside time, or social time, or video-game time for reading time. *The Diary*, by stark contrast, does all of that and more: It opens an avenue for students to talk to each other about literature and about heavy themes handled with a light touch.

The savvy teacher elicits and unpacks these themes, never skimming over the crucial features of the text that allow readers to move past the surface comedy and spectatorship that propel us through the plot. These themes — themes of adolescence, racism, loss, family, redemption, friendship, and prejudice — touch nearly every aspect of this text. The book opens up an American experience with nuance, humanity, and honesty, one about American Indians, who are nearly always invisible in contemporary American culture.

When I save *The Diary* for the end of the year, many students lament that I didn't assign them such good books all year long. I agree, dear students: Sometimes in my desire to teach important lessons, I select the classics, and these texts aren't always as compelling as this delicious Alexie novel. My best response is that if you eat your lima beans, you earn your dessert.

And now, dear readers, I hope you, too, enjoyed your dessert.

—Anna Baldwin
English teacher, Arlee High School
Arlee, Montana

A comic strip inspired by *The Absolutely True Diary of a Part-Time Indian,* by Emilia Burkhart, student, age 11.

STORY BY SHERMAN ALEXIE, WRITING AND ILLUSTRATION BY EMILA BURKHART.

PAGE 269

The first chapter from an early draft of *The Absolutely True Diary of a Part-Time Indian*, originally titled **Water on the Brain**

CHAPTER 1

Let me introduce you to the Spokane Indian Reservation.

First of all, the place is all pine trees, pine trees, pine trees. And then, after you look past all of those pine trees, you can see more pine trees. And after you walk past those trees, you run into a few more. If you picked up a rock, closed your eyes, and tossed the rock in any direction, you'd be a superhero surrounded by gazillions of untossed pine trees.

I hate pine trees.

Yeah, sure, they're beautiful, I guess, in a pine-tree sort of way, all green and thin and tall, but there's such a thing as *too much beauty*. You can be suffocated by beauty just like you can be suffocated by water.

And yes, there is *too much water* on my reservation.

There are gazillions of lakes and ponds, meaning there are also gazillions upon gazillions of mosquitoes. I read somewhere that an insect is born every time a human commits a sin, so that means we Spokane Indians are very busy.

The Columbia River — one of the largest, most powerful, and most radioactive rivers *in the whole dang world* — forms one border of our reservation, which is shaped like a clumsy, incomplete triangle. The Spokane River forms the second border, and Tshimikain Creek forms the third side. Now, geographically speaking, the rez is not an island, but you still have to cross bridges to get to us. And yes, we Indians have to cross those same bridges to get out, so there's definitely a whole lot of bridge-crossing on the rez.

I hate bridges.

But I hate mountains more. And I can't stand canyons, either. Fields of wildflowers make me sneeze. And don't get me started on starry, starry nights.

Cougars, bears, and moose have walked through the middle of Wellpinit, the capital of the reservation. An elk once stood at my bedroom window and stared at me. And, hey, you nature lovers are probably excited about these animal encounters, but I'd like to teach you a lesson about wildlife. And maybe you'll pay more attention to me because I live in the woods. I don't like cougars and bears because *they eat people*. And I don't like elk because they smell dead. And I absolutely hate moose because they are the biggest, meanest jerks in the entire world. Moose have bad tempers. Moose spit on you. Moose pee and poop on you. Moose will chase you down and stomp you to death. Bears and cougars are scared of moose. Heck, except for mating, moose wander through the wilderness alone because they don't even like each other. There is nobody that hates moose more than another moose. You draw a mustache on a moose and it will turn into Saddam Hussein.

If you learn only one thing from my story, I hope it is this: STAY AWAY FROM MOOSE!

I know that sensitive and kind people are supposed to go dizzy over nature.

They're supposed to get out guitars and drums, organize themselves into sacred circles, and *write terrible songs*. Some people look at a sunrise or a narrow ridge or a snow-covered field or a moose and they cry. No, they *weep with joy* because they're so much more poetic than the rest of us.

Poets drool over golden wheat and impossible clouds and birds in flight. But birds don't fly because it's romantic. They fly because they have to. If they could figure out a faster way to travel, I'm sure the birds would go for it. But they're *just birds*. Don't get me wrong. I like most birds, and I think hummingbirds are way cool, but I don't get all misty-eyed about their wings. Birds use flight like humans use hammers and nails. Do birds write romantic poems about carpenters? Maybe if the carpenter has built a kick-butt bird feeder.

I once read a poem where the poet dude talked about a tiger like he wanted to marry it. What kind of guy wants to marry a tiger? A goofy poet!

I hate poets.

Okay, so you're probably wondering if I hate everything. You're probably thinking that I'm one of those angry kids who only know how to complain. But that's not true at all. In fact, I don't really hate pine trees or water. I just hate being poor, and when you're living in poverty in a place filled with pine trees and water, you start blaming the trees and rivers for your poverty. It's easier to hate a pine tree than to hate the government. It's easier to cuss at a river than to cuss at the president.

And you must never, never, never, never, never blame your parents for your poverty, no matter how many jobs they lose or how much money they spend on beer and cigars and broken cars, because your mother and father are like gravity and oxygen and your world will EXPLODE without them.

But the number one bad thing about being poor is the feeling that you somehow *deserve* to be poor. You start believing that you're poor because you are stupid and ugly. And then you start believing that you're stupid and ugly because you're Indian. And because you're Indian you start believing you're destined to be poor. It's an ugly circle, and *there's nothing you can do about it*.

Poverty doesn't give you strength or teach you lessons about perseverance. No, poverty only teaches you how to be poor.

And now you're probably thinking, "Hey, buddy, if you're *so aware* of your problems, if you're so *freaking smart*, then why don't you do something about them? Huh, buddy, huh? And, by the way, I think moose are pretty cool."

Well, I once read that human beings are hardwired like computers. Sure, you can shove gigabytes of software into a computer, but that doesn't really change the hardware. The *essence* of the computer will never change. And I don't think human beings change, no matter how many gigabytes of happy thoughts and happier pills you shove down our throats.

What it comes down to is this: You don't have many choices when you're poor, and choiceless people are unhappy people. I think it is completely *impossible* to be poor and happy.

Oh, I know that a gazillion different politicians and philosophers have said, "Money doesn't solve all of your problems." But they're *lying*. It's been scientifically proven that money will solve most of your problems and give you a fighting chance at the rest of them.

Have you ever noticed that the only people who say that money isn't everything are the people who already have plenty of money?

And, okay, I know that sounds hateful, like I'm some communist rebel trying to stick it to THE MAN, but I don't even know who THE MAN is. Though I've got the sneaking suspicion that

THE MAN lives in a nice house with an intelligent wife and talented children and they all have *enough food to eat*, so I think I'd rather be and eat like THE MAN than hate THE MAN.

Trust me, I'd rather love and be loved. I am not a hateful person. I'm just a poor Indian kid who wants to have a better life. A great life. *An amazing life.*

And I know you're probably thinking, "How can a dirt-poor reservation kid live an amazing life?" Well, to tell the truth, I don't have a clue where to begin. But I want the amazing; I want it so bad, so maybe *the wanting* is the beginning. Maybe wanting is the beginning of every story.

Think about it. Adam and Eve wanted to smooch. Hamlet wanted to avenge his father. Harriet Tubman wanted freedom. Luke Skywalker wanted to find his father.

But I'm getting carried away with all the hating and the wanting. I want you to like me, maybe even to love me. Heck, we all want to be liked and loved. But you can't jump around like a stray dog and tell people that you want to be liked and loved. And past the age of ten, you certainly can't ask to be liked or loved. That's just desperate.

But, hey, wait a minute, *I am desperate.* So what can I do to make you love me? Should I pull a rabbit out of a hat? Read poems to you? Juggle chainsaws? Draw cartoons?

I drew a cartoon just for you. Does it make you happy? Or sad? Or just plain confused? Well, let me make something clear. I am happy and sad and confused all at the same time. I always feel clumsy. No, I always feel awkward. "Awkward" is a better word. "Awkward" is the perfect word for what I feel like. And I always feel like I'm going to bump into something and break my collarbone or my heart.

But there I go again, talking about my life like it's a soap opera. And I hate soap operas.

So I must confess that my life on the rez is not so horrible. It's actually pretty decent. If I had to guess, I'd say my life is about 52 percent good and 48 percent bad, and that's a dang good score in a world where approximately 90 percent of the people are 90 percent sad. So I should probably stop whining. After all, I am loved and I do love. And I'll prove it, too. These are the eight things that I love with all my heart and soul:

1. my grandmother
2. my mother and father (the parental units count as one)
3. my big sister
4. math (especially geometry)
5. my best friend
6. drawing cartoons
7. any sport involving a ball
8. the beautiful girl named X

Jess Walter Interviews Sherman Alexie

Note: This interview has been abridged. The full interview is available in the audiobook edition.

Sherman Alexie: Hello, everybody, this is Sherman Alexie. I'm sitting in the studio with Jess Walter, and we're going to have a discussion about the tenth anniversary edition of *The Absolutely True Diary of a Part-Time Indian*. I'm laughing because I just did an event in Oregon and the Oregon State librarian couldn't remember the title and called it *The Partially Part-Time True Story of a Full-Time Worker* or something....[*Laughs*] I get into trouble with my long titles.

Jess Walter: [*Laughs*] And I'm Jess Walter, I'm Sherman's long-time friend and cohost of *A Tiny Sense of Accomplishment*, the hardest-to-find podcast in the world, as we like to think of it. It's such an honor to be here talking about your unfortunately titled book that has done so poorly over this last decade.

SA: Yeah, I mean…I wish I had written a book that sold more copies and got more attention.

JW: And that sadly had just a little bit of influence on the culture. I don't know how many times I came around the corner to see one of my kids reading it for school.

SA: [*Laughs*] Oh man. My kid read it for school, which is the most bizarre thing. My poor son. It was the book of the first quint of his sixth-grade year, and he protested, though, in a way. He agreed to read it as long as no one asked him questions, like the teacher or the students, and no one got to interrogate him about the book or about me. But he got a C. I think it was a gentleman's C. It was his protest C.

JW: That's a great protest, to get a C on your dad's book. I think that's the kind of rebellion we can all live with.

SA: I was very proud of him.

JW: It's funny, you probably get this from people who ask about your books, "Which one's your favorite?" And in the authors' union, it says you have to say, "My books are all like children, they're all exactly the same." But on the tenth birthday of this one, you have to admit the reach of this book is probably unlike any that you've written before.

SA: There're only a few books that remain positive, that I remain positive about, and *True Diary* is at the top of that list. I very much…I didn't know what I was writing. I've had a great career completely apart from *True Diary*. But this has gone…I won the Peter Pan Prize for Young Adult Literature in Scandinavia. I mean, the green tights looked great on me at the awards ceremonies.

JW: If you're going to win the Peter Pan Prize, I would think it would be for not growing up.

SA: [*Laughs*] So, the international reach, the fact that it's taught in *thousands* of high schools…I still get letters. Ten years later, I still get letters from high school students. I'm meeting people who are college graduates who read it in junior high.

JW: Ten years, and reaching out to young readers that way — we know some great readers, but those young readers, the power the book holds on them, a book like this, it must be really profound to hear from them.

SA: Well, think of the books that we read when we were kids and how formative they are. I think of *It* by Stephen King or *The Snowy Day* when I was much younger, the picture book by Ezra Jack Keats. I didn't have imaginary playmates growing up like some kids did; I had books. Books were my imaginary playmates. Books were my siblings and sometimes books were the best version of a parent I could have. So to think I might have even a fraction of that power for a kid with *True Diary* is amazing.

JW: You must see it. I see kids carrying the book around. You must get letters from kids that just blow you away.

SA: The most powerful ones are the ones I get from the teachers or the kids themselves about reluctant readers. The thing I hear all the time is, "This is the first book I ever finished," which is on one level very sad, an indictment of our education system, but on the other level, you think, well, maybe I'm the gateway book, the gateway drug. Maybe my book will lead this kid into other books. But to have had that influence on somebody who didn't like books, who didn't like to read and then all of a sudden I get these letters from these kids: "This is the first book I've finished." "I stole it from the library." I get very excited. And teachers write me letters and say, "I can't keep this in my classroom because all these kids steal it."

JW: Oh, that's so great.

SA: One of the great moments for me was maybe about six or seven years ago, I read in New York and this entire class of kids from the Bronx came. It was a public school in the Bronx, so it was all brown kids of various ethnicities and races and countries, you know, a lot of them are first-generation immigrants. It was really amazing to see this incredibly diverse group of kids so identify with this reservation Indian boy. And you know, we're from the same place in the world, I mean, Eastern Washington from Springdale and Wellpinit, from the rez and just off the rez, and to think that we could have any standing or any influence over *anybody*, let alone some kid in the Bronx? It's astonishing. It never fails to astonish me.

JW: But I think that's the universal quality of books written for teens up to young adults, is that idea…the universal. I remember reading *A Wrinkle in Time* and you know, my dad wasn't a professor, but you identify with those kids. You identify with Charlie going into the chocolate factory. You become that character, and

I think that's what that book's done so amazingly. I spoke at an alternative school, and the first question I get from this kid is, "Do you know Sherman Alexie?" "No, I never met him." "That's the only book I ever read; I *love* that book."

SA: [*Laughs*]

JW: Again, here's a kid with a tough childhood. That has to be a recurring theme you hear over the last ten years.

SA: I mean, books saved me, so I think *True Diary* might be part of the emergency kit for a lot of students. One of the things I hear, too, now, is, "This book led me to become a writer. I'm in this MFA program because of *Absolutely True Diary of a Part-Time Indian*."

JW: Do you remember when Arnold Spirit first, when that voice first…Books come in voices, and the voice here is so strong, I had to think that the voice is what popped in your head.

SA: Well, it's autobiographical, of course, but he's a much more confident person than I was at the same age. And he's really also kinder.

JW: It's funny, as I read it — you know, you had become a father — I thought you were looking at fatherhood through your boys' eyes, both the kindness and the savvy of your two sons.

SA: My sons are urban Indians, they are very much urban kids so they have urban skills and they're also members of this generation who are much more self-aware and aware of the world, and they *are* kinder. My sons at the same age are *far* kinder than I was, partly because their survival is assured right now, and mine wasn't. So I think Arnold Spirit Jr. has less of the cannibalistic instincts I did. It's less Donner Party for him than it was for me.

JW: I think sometimes my kids doubt the *Lord of the Flies* nature of the stories I tell. I mean, the bus stop was as horrifying a place as could exist. I mean, it was Dante's fourth circle.

SA: [*Laughs*] The public school bus stop. Yeah.

JW: It is hard to get across. But it seems like the voice, while autobiographical, also does seem of itself. You have no doubt of who Junior is in this book. He seems fully realized from the beginning.

SA: In a lot of ways, I think I created the idealized version of me. A lot of wish fulfillment on who I wish I would have been back then, or maybe looking back, decisions I would have made or ways I would have acted. I could have been a better person, slightly better. And also in writing the other characters, I blended people, I took real aspects of certain people and blended them into a fictional stew and created these other characters. It's realistic and people are racist and classist and sexist and mean and funny and kind. And I think because I wrote with specific people in mind, it was easier to create a real world or a fictional world that felt real.

JW: Has the response in that real world been different than to your other books?

SA: You know, I never really heard much from Reardan. I mean, there's a real Gordy—Gordy the white boy genius in the book—there's a real character he's based on. He had a different name in the early drafts; I think I called him Henry?

JW: Oh, and it just never felt right, I guess.

SA: No, and I sent the manuscript to the real Gordy, and he said, "Yeah, this is good, but why are you calling him Henry? Call him Gordy." So he wanted his real name in the book. To this day I think he's the only real person I've seen at a reading of *True Diary*. He lives in Arizona and I gave a reading in Arizona, and I knew he was coming, but I didn't have a cell phone back then so I had no contact with him, and I was reading the book and I decided to read that chapter — even though I hadn't seen him yet — where Gordy teaches Arnold about books and boners and how to read and the importance of education....That's also an interesting thing to write in the book, that positive idea of education. I think that was quietly revolutionary for a Native American character.

JW: It really is a quest to have the best education you can get.

SA: It's the *Iliad* of public school education, the *Odyssey* of public school education. And I was reading the chapter and I was getting emotional just thinking about Gordy being out there, not seeing him yet, and then as I was reading I looked up and we locked eyes and he was in the crowd and he was *weeping*....I mean, his shoulders were shaking and tears were running down his face. To see somebody I had written about and somebody who meant so much to me from my past and somebody who *did* become part of that group I ended up in — where education was *so* valued, where education was seen as a great path, where there was this heroic quality to it, to the idea of going to college, to aspiring to intellectualism, to aspiring to academic achievement — to be a successful writer having gone through that path and succeeded in all sorts of ways and then to look in the crowd and see my old friend, who had also succeeded intellectually...to be the men we've become and to look across that room and remember the kids we were, it was really incredible.

JW: That need and ability to fight for your own education — that's another universal thing. I look at where we are now…Kids are going to have to take all the belligerence, all the anger, everything they have, and turn it toward their own education.

SA: I mean, look, I collected aluminum cans one summer to pay for the SAT prep course — aluminum *beer* cans on the rez to pay for my SAT prep course.

JW: And you ended up buying two cars. [*Laughs*]

SA: I built a car out of empty beer cans. [*Laughs*] And so I think this book's subtext, and text, in celebrating education is huge, and I think that's one of the reasons why it's so big and why it does so well, is that it does it in a funny way. It's a celebration of high school education with dick jokes.

JW: Right, right. What could be more subversive than that? [*Laughs*] In the last ten years, of course, a lot of other things have changed, and there's another character in the book, Rowdy, who was also based on a real friend. I think I told you I reread the ending of the book and it was so poignant — Junior and Rowdy talking about seeing each other as old men.

SA: Yeah. As those of you reading this tenth anniversary edition know when you read the afterword, Rowdy was based on my childhood best friend, Randy Peone — I really dramatically changed that name, from Randy to Rowdy…

JW: Two letters!

SA: Fooled everybody on the rez. [*Laughs*]

He died in a car wreck in December of 2016. And the question...When you sent me that e-mail saying you had re-read it, I hadn't reread the book, not the ending, and when you asked that question that they ask of each other, "Are we going to know each other as old men?" — when I wrote it in 2006, when I was working on the book, of course I always imagined that Randy and I would know each other as old men. I'm still in mourning; I mean, it's only been a few months since he died. And I'm not just mourning him and our friendship. I'm mourning the way in which maybe we would have reunited and reconciled in some small or large way. I'm mourning the loss of possibilities.

JW: There's something about those eleven-, twelve-year-old friendships, when you're at that age where you've seen the best and the worst of each other and you've made it through something together. You do root for them.

SA: That's what he did. He, more than any other person outside of my parents and siblings, gave me permission and celebrated my leaving. He never punished me for it, not after that first year. That first year he punished me, but we reconciled after that. And even now, especially now that he's gone, as I doubt my journey away from the rez, my continuing journey away from the rez — I know that he always supported me, if not in presence or if not in postcards or phone calls, I know that he was happy for me.

JW: And in a way that allowed you to go find who you were, to express yourself, to live.

SA: I was not a courageous boy when he first moved to Wellpinit, but I left Wellpinit in a courageous way and I owe a huge debt to Randy for that courage.

JW: Junior's art, his drawings — was that a way to sort of allegorically write about your own writing? How did you decide he would be the funny artist that he is?

SA: So I wrote the book, and immediately I made him a cartoonist, in the first paragraph, in the first draft, on the first hour of writing, I made him a cartoonist. And part of it was, while working on my movie *The Business of Fancydancing*, I became good friends with one of the crew members who was friends with Ellen Forney, who ended up doing the art. I made him a cartoonist and I thought, of course Ellen Forney — this thirtysomething alternative bisexual woman from Philadelphia — can channel a fifteen-year-old reservation Indian boy. Of course, of course, of course. And I think even now, sometimes I hear from Natives wondering why I didn't choose a Native: "Why didn't you choose a Native artist? Why didn't you choose a Native artist?" I wasn't that conscious of the decision then, but looking back I realize that at the beginning of the creative process, if it had been a Native artist, they would have had too many opinions. [*Laughs*] They would have! They would have had their own ideas.

JW: Because Ellen's illustrations are so perfect, but they come so much out of the text. It's like watching a great actor inhabit a role.

SA: That's what happened. The first third I dictated to her. I dictated in the book, I dictated over the phone, I dictated in person. So I was really in charge of all the illustrations at the beginning. And then it slowly became collaborative. And then by the end, the last third of the illustrations, she was coming up with her own ideas. She came to inhabit that character from an outside perspective, so I think my insider perspective and her outsider perspective combined to create this original character.

JW: And in the end, Arnold talks again a little bit about the different tribes we can belong to. By the end, and having met Ellen, she —

SA: She belongs to a thousand tribes at once.

JW: She does!

SA: I had never even thought about it that way — my collaboration with a white person, with a white woman, echoing the collaboration of Junior inside the novel. It never even occurred to me, Jess.

JW: Yes, it did.

SA: No, it never did. It never did. It never even occurred that my artistic collaboration with Ellen Forney mirrored Junior's collaboration and introduction to the white world through the white kids in Reardan.

JW: Another question I know you've gotten over the last ten years is about the movie. And whether there'll be one.

SA: Well, immediately there was interest in the book, and I said no. And at the same time I was angry about saying no and angry there wasn't a movie because we Natives are so screwed in Hollywood by representation, by inaccurate and racist misrepresentations, just crappy movies, and I didn't want to go through the process. I mean, I've been working in Hollywood since *Smoke Signals*. I worked on my own projects that never got made, I worked on other people's projects that never got made. So the constant demoralizing failure to get anything made and dealing with Hollywood and the hypocrisy of all these Hollywood liberals behaving like rapacious Wall Street capitalists at all times, and the racism and sexism and homophobia of the most supposedly liberal community in the world — Hollywood — so all of that, there was just no way. Twice, all I had to do was sign a contract and I would have had a movie deal. And I said no. Never in my life has anything felt more like signing a treaty than trying to sign a movie deal with Hollywood. Never have I felt more compromised and in danger morally than signing a movie deal with Hollywood.

JW: Were you feeling protective about the book itself, about Junior and his story — that either they won't make it or they'll get it wrong?

SA: Yeah, that it would end up in the maw of nothingness, the factory of nothing being produced where it just cycles, it's on the spin cycle in the Hollywood washing machine forever and ever.

JW: So initially you say no out of frustration with Hollywood and to protect the story.

SA: And to protect myself and the characters of my own story. And so for a decade I said no, I said no. And very recently, a team started courting me, and so I said yes. [*Laughs*] And as we're recording this, as we're having this conversation, I have the contracts in hand.

JW: So we're at that place of signing again?

SA: [*Laughs*] I'm in that place now, signing again. I love the producers, they're great. I've enjoyed their respectful take. It feels like Hollywood has changed...for me. Briefly. Maybe. But then who knows?

JW: The fear always would be, what if Junior is an Irish kid. You know, or...?

SA: Well, I have protections put in place where only Native American actors or First Nations will play the Native American characters in my book, in the movie. And it's by my definitions, the approvals are based on *my* definitions of what Native American and First Nations is, because there are all sorts of folks who claim Indian-ness and there're all sorts of Native American — in five-inch-thick parentheses — who claim to be Native in the acting world. So by my definitions, by the author and executive producer of *The Absolutely True Diary of a Part-Time Indian* movie, I get to choose who gets to be in the movie.

JW: And you're involved...you're writing the script?

SA: I'm writing the script. I'm a producer. Directing is a possibility.

JW: So hopefully with that protection in place...You think about how many lives the book has touched, and we know that there are some kids who still don't get to books. You must know with *Smoke Signals* the reach a film can have. It must be exciting — as writers we're not made to be optimists, and as a reservation Indian, you're especially not — but the idea that a film could come out of it and reach that many more people, young people especially, must be thrilling.

SA: Twenty years since *Smoke Signals*, the first movie I made, has been out, and I would be in an airport, I was in a Chicago airport once and I heard from across the distance, "Hey, Victor."

JW: "Hey, Victor." [*Laughs*]

SA: So I am highly aware that movies have a lot more cultural power and a lot more political power than books do. And especially in this Internet era? To think that this movie plays theaters hopefully and then hits Netflix…No matter how well it does in the theaters, it's going to hit Netflix eventually, or whatever Netflix becomes, or whatever competition to Netflix might arise.

JW: Now, writing the script yourself puts a different kind of pressure on, because *Absolutely True Diary* is the favorite book of so many people. I mean, that's their favorite book, and you had better be faithful, or get it right, or nail it. Do you feel that? Are you going to feel that from readers?

SA: I'm a chronic rewriter. So the producers actually had to rein me in, to stick more with the book. I was willing to change everything. My first draft of the screenplay, it was set in an Amish community.

JW: [*Laughs*] "The scene where Junior becomes a Jedi, we're a little confused by…"

SA: So I am perfectly willing to change everything, so long as it's my decision. But they reined me back in, and it is very faithful to the book.

JW: Oh, good. Can you imagine that first reader coming up to you and saying —

SA: Saying, "I hate the movie, you broke my heart."

JW: "You've ruined your own book, Mister Alexie."

SA: It's going to happen. And also in the Native American world, the Internet has made the tribalism and the tribal peer pressure even greater. The movie is going to become a big thing, a big cultural moment. And I can't even imagine the ways in which it's going to be judged harshly by the Native American intellectual world, who are going to be nitpicking it. I think of *Thunder Boy Jr.*, my picture book which was published, and one page was about a kid dreaming of a powwow and there were critiques that it wasn't an accurate representation of a powwow because there were three drums and animals were drumming. There're not three drums at a powwow.

JW: Do you know how hard it is to teach an animal to drum, to keep the same rhythm?

SA: [*Laughs*] So at readings, I've been mocking those Native American critics, those fundamentalists, by saying, "I have to speak to all you non-Natives in the crowd that if you do happen to attend a powwow expecting — because of my picture book — to see a bear, a coyote, and a snake drumming, it's not going to happen. Now, you might see three drummers nicknamed Bear, Coyote, and Snake, but you're not going to see the actual animals, so I'm sorry for that cultural misrepresentation. I'm sorry if I've given you a stereotypical racist example of what could happen at a powwow." *True Diary* got some of that also ten years ago, but the culture has changed so dramatically in terms of not just judging non-Native representations of Native-ness, but harshly judging Native representations of ourselves. This is *my* story, this stuff actually happened to me, and I get judged for telling the story of the real-life decisions I made.

JW: I wondered about that, that's another thing in the last decade, if Native American representations in films and books have changed in some way, or if those battles are still fought in the same way.

SA: We're still underrepresented in every art form. You know, I was in New York recently and doing an interview, we're in MoMA, that was part of the interview, and I was walking through MoMA, and I said every museum in the country could also be called the Museum That Excludes Native American Thought. That could be the subtitle of every museum in the country.

So the fact remains that we are not seen as contemporary. And the sneaky thing about colonialism is that I think far too many indigenous peoples don't think of themselves as being contemporary. In fact, they all too often romanticize their own past. I think nostalgia is a terminal condition among the indigenous. In writing this book, and now in working on the movie, and in my whole career, I would hope to be indigenous nostalgia's greatest enemy. I hope that's on my tombstone. I want that on my tombstone.

JW: I want to talk to you about *Diary* showing up on so many banned books list. And didn't it finally drop off?

SA: It was in the top ten for nine years, but it never made number one. I was always number two. The two books that always kept me out were: *Captain Underpants*...So one year *Captain Underpants* was more dangerous than my book. All the conservative book banners of the country decided that *Captain Underpants* was more dangerous than *True Diary*. And then another year it was *And Tango Makes Three*, which is about the gay penguins in the Bronx Zoo. So apparently, gay penguins and *Captain Underpants* are more politically dangerous than a reservation Indian boy seeking a better education.

JW: It's given you in many ways the chance to rail about intellectual freedom, and about kids and the things they read, and about freedom of speech. It's given you this platform in a way. Every time they ban the book, I think —

SA: Every time they ban the book, it becomes national headlines. I sell more books, so it's actually lucrative for me. We call Banned Books Week in my house "Big-Assed Royalties Week."

On a personal level that happens, but it ended up happening that I was often asked to speak about censorship. I was talking with a friend, and the thing is, I feel most indigenous when I'm asked to speak on nonindigenous subjects, or not-exclusively indigenous subjects, so as a Spokane Indian writer, when I'm asked to speak about censorship, I feel *most* Indian, because I don't have to talk about being Indian. What I do is…The brain I have, which has been acculturated Spokane, which has been acculturated Native American, which has been acculturated contemporary indigenous filtered through all these American experiences, is who I am. So I get to be who I *am*, so getting censored makes me feel like they're censoring me the individual, and that makes me so happy. They're picking on *me*.

JW: I wonder if you ever heard from young readers about the issues of adults. I mean, adults are afraid that kids might see the word "boner" or read about masturbation or things that, of course, no high school kid has ever thought about in the history of time.

SA: Well, in various places, kids actually led the efforts against the bans. In Boise, Idaho, this young woman actually led the effort. She ended up in a city park distributing copies of *True Diary* to the public to battle against her own school board. So I've gotten letters from all sorts of kids like that who are fighting their own parents. Even last night at my son's school, there was a man who was a liberal — it's a very liberal school in a very liberal city — and we were talking about the influence of culture on our children and he advocated getting rid of your television, and I just shook my head. I mean, what a cliché, number one. And also, how censorious. What a censorious impulse. Does that man even recognize his own censorious impulses? That he wants to get rid of the outside world. That he wants to get rid of any image, any idea, any story, any thought that might upset him, that might cause him to have a conversation with his own child. Or, "Oh my God, there's going to be something on that box I disagree with. Oh my God, I have to stop that." Book banning punishes the imagination. Book banning punishes dialogue. Book banning turns disagreement into something evil and unwanted. Book banning turns opposing ideas into sins. Book banning is fundamentally religious, regardless of the religion. And I'm a secular warrior for free speech.

JW: The book has given you so many opportunities to speak to communities about that, too.

SA: Oh yeah, it's been amazing, and it's also so cute and quaint. It actually makes me feel so positive about books. That people are still so afraid of books that they'll ban a book, they'll keep their kid from reading a book, and yet their kid has an iPhone in their hands, access to every porn site in the world, access to all the porn that has ever been created, and yet they want my book banned because a teenage boy twice mentions masturbation. I think it says something about books still being far more powerful. That the written word is still far more powerful than people think it is.

JW: That immersion, that their kids are not just going to see pictures, they're going to get ideas.

SA: Yes, yes, yes. Scary books. Scary books.

JW: This was your first YA book. Did it cause you to look at that genre differently? Read differently?

SA: *True Diary* coincided with this rise in young adult literature. I mean, *Harry Potter* was a kids' book. When you look back at the chronology of *Harry Potter*, I don't think there's ever been a more dramatic example of somebody getting better, getting so much better as a writer in the public eye, like the *dramatic* increase. The first couple of *Harry Potter* books are very much children's books, but as they went on, as the kids got older, and as J. K. Rowling got more experience, the books became…I mean, they're biblical. Holy crap, they're biblical. I'm going to argue right here that I think the *Harry Potter* books and the movies combined are more important in American culture than any other book or any other TV show, any other cultural phenomenon. I think they have more spiritual power, I think they have more political power, more *everything*. The first one came out in 1998, which is incredible when you think about *Harry Potter*. But my career and my thoughts about young adult were right in the middle of all that and so when young adult literature exploded — *The Hunger Games*; John Green; *Thirteen Reasons Why*, which is like the massive thing on Netflix right now — I accidentally became part of this amazing new phenomenon, the young adult book being a universally praised and admired genre.

It remains the bestselling genre. If you want to sell books as a writer, write young adult.

JW: And it seems like another boundary or border was crossed, because adult readers, of course, came along, but it also said kids can handle six hundred pages, they can handle dialogue about masturbation. It also stopped underestimating the fifteen-year-old reader, the thirteen-year-old reader.

SA: It stopped being condescending.

It really is a form of political rebellion. Young readers becoming political rebels by insisting on their own genre. When *The Outsiders* was published, nobody thought about it as being young adult. When *The Catcher in the Rye* was published, nobody thought about it as being young adult. *Lord the Flies, Tom Sawyer, Huckleberry Finn*…when we talk about so many of the great books of our past, they would be classified as young adult now. And that would be a great thing.

We all became writers because of something we read when we were twelve. And I get to be that guy. It's awesome.

Interview with Ellen Forney

How long have you been drawing comics?

I've drawn pictures from as far back as I can remember, but I didn't start drawing narrative comics until I was in high school. I drew a full-page comic for a friend who had quit her job at the ice cream parlor where we both worked — the piece was called "The Trials and Tribulations of Tina-Beena," and included a bunch of little stories about the way South Philly girls pronounced "Oreos" and the time she argued with a customer — stuff like that. She loved it and hung it up in her kitchen under a piece of plastic wrap.

How did you and Sherman work together?

Sherman would give me a few chapters of his manuscript and ideas for what I might draw, and I'd do thumbnail sketches using his list as a bouncing-off point. Later, we'd go over what I'd come up with. About a third of the graphics were Sherman's ideas, a third were real collaborations, and a third were my ideas that struck me as I read the text.

How was it getting into the head of Arnold Spirit?

Intense. Sherman describes Arnold so well in the text that I felt I had a good grip on who Arnold was. But to draw like him, to think of jokes that he might tell, I had to really immerse myself in being him, and it wasn't an easy place to be.

For instance, while drawing my last round of thumbnail sketches, I was working in a café, with manuscripts and sketches spread out all over the table. I'd worked for hours, hadn't eaten in a long time, and I drank too much coffee. I was deep in Arnold's head and felt like I had to keep going. So much heavy stuff was happening in the story, that's when I came up with some of Arnold's darkest humor, like the comic about the last sip of wine and the *Burning Love* book cover cartoon when Arnold's sister died.

Then when I got to the end of the manuscript, where Arnold and Rowdy play basketball, and as it was getting dark outside, I felt a tightening in my chest and I realized I was about to bawl. It felt like I was playing a bittersweet basketball game with Rowdy. I had a split second to decide whether or not I would cry in the café, and I put my head in my hands, sobbed once, and thought about something else. I had read that section so many times, but until then I hadn't been so deep in Arnold's mind.

What was your biggest concern/objective when creating the art for the book?

My absolute biggest concern was to make Arnold's comics look authentic. I was afraid my work would look too polished and professional, or maybe too goofy, but I also didn't want to dumb it down or stiffen it up. I briefly tried to draw like some of my teenage boy students, but that didn't work at all — you could tell I was trying too hard and it was obvious that it wasn't my style. So I talked about it with Sherman, and he thought it'd be fine if I just drew like me.

What's the most difficult part of the process: sketching the artwork or inking?

My process for this book was different from usual. In most of my work, doing the thumbnails is hard (writing and drawing my brainstorming ideas), sketching is easier (penciling and polishing up what I've laid out in the thumbnails), and inking is easiest (I use a brush and india ink).

For this book, the thumbnails were hard because I had to stay in Arnold's mindset, and I was interpreting someone else's work. Sketching was weird because I had to remember to keep the looseness of the thumbnails, and inking was REALLY HARD! The drawings needed to look like Arnold just sat down and drew them, boom. This may sound counterintuitive, but it takes way more concentration and confidence to make fast lines and swoops than my usual slow and deliberate inking. Also, Arnold wouldn't use a brush in his sketchbook, so I used a felt-tip pen. So not only was I using an unfamiliar tool, I was trying to make labored drawings look spontaneous. I got cramps in my hand a lot.

Why did you use so many different drawing styles?

I used three drawing styles. In my own sketchbooks (and scraps of paper and backs of envelopes), I use different styles for different purposes, and I felt that Arnold would, too. Arnold's artwork needed to span different situations and moods, so his drawing style needed change as well.

First, the more scribbled-looking illustrations and comics suggest that Arnold is jotting down his thoughts in an immediate way, like he'd just had an idea and quickly wrote it down. Most of the artwork is like that.

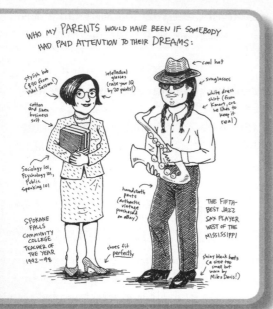

WHO MY PARENTS WOULD HAVE BEEN IF SOMEBODY HAD PAID ATTENTION TO THEIR DREAMS:

Stylish bob ($50 from Vidal Sassoon!)

cotton and linen business suit

intellectual glasses (raise your IQ by 20 points!)

Sociology 101, Psychology 101, Public Speaking 101

SPOKANE FALLS COMMUNITY COLLEGE TEACHER OF THE YEAR 1992-98

shoes fit perfectly

cool hat

sunglasses

white dress shirt (from Kmart, cuz he likes to keep it real)

houndstooth pants (authentic vintage purchased on eBay)

THE FIFTH-BEST JAZZ SAX PLAYER WEST OF THE MISSISSIPPI

shiny black boots (a size too small but worn by Miles Davis!)

Second, the slightly more realistic cartoons, like the annotated portraits of his family, suggest that he's giving more thought to what he's doing. Certain ideas would have been rumbling around his head and were well-developed by the time he put them on the page.

Third, the penciled portraits suggest two different types of intimate situations. Detailed, more realistic drawings can take a while, and in that way describe a span of time, so we know that Arnold was concentrating and focusing on his artwork and on whatever subject he was drawing.

Gordy
(+ metaphysical humor)

The pencil sketches of his friends suggest that he spent a lot of time with his friends looking at them intently and that they were comfortable with that intimacy. For example, I imagined that Arnold sketched his friend Gordy as he studied in the library, concentrating on the weird way Gordy rested his face on his hand with his intent facial expression and the curve of his shoulders. Arnold was using his sketchbook to love Gordy, in a way.

Other pencil sketches, like the portrait of Eugene on a motorcycle, suggest that he drew them from a photograph. He wanted to spend time with those people, but for some reason — logistically, or emotionally — couldn't do it in person.

One other detailed style was for the Penelope bird. When Arnold drew that, he was thinking about how he loved Penelope and how they both wanted to fly away. I thought he might sit with that feeling for a while and I imagined he was in the school library copying a bird out of a textbook. Arnold would sit and draw very meditatively in ink — all the feathers, using shading, crosshatching, and even little dots.

Can you explain how the portrait of Rowdy evolved from being a straight-on elegant sketch to one that was defaced?
I actually did a similar thing in one of my own sketchbooks several years ago. I was in a terrible mood, and was drawing a self-portrait to get it out of my system. I was about half-done and I hated it, so I scribbled a big "X" over my whole face. When I looked at it later, I realized that it reflected my mood much better than if I'd actually finished the drawing.

The drawing of Rowdy is meant to be a vignette, describing the particular intimacy in Arnold and Rowdy's friendship. Rowdy was much more defensive than Arnold about how close they were, and was constantly pulling Arnold to him and pushing him away, often at the same time. I pictured the scene like this:

Rowdy was lying on the floor in an unself-conscious way. Arnold was sneakily drawing a portrait of him, but when Arnold was only half-done, Rowdy looked up and snapped, "What're you drawing?!" The scene changed from intimacy to defensiveness with Arnold stopping and scribbling the cartoon face over Rowdy's face, with the word balloon of Rowdy's verbal slap.

I hadn't planned all that out when I started doing the sketch, but when I was half-done, I realized that Arnold wouldn't have been able to pin Rowdy down for very long. I took a piece of tracing paper and scribbled an angry cartoon face over Rowdy's face, and that looked just right to me.

What do you feel is the biggest contribution your artwork brings to the book?

Arnold depends on his cartoons to express himself, be understood, to escape, and to survive. He says they are his "tiny little lifeboats." The reader needs to see what he's talking about and what he means by that.

Drawing in your own sketchbook is like writing in your own diary, which is very personal. And creative people can do some intense work when they're using their medium to express themselves, just for themselves. Arnold doesn't even understand all these things he's getting down on paper, because so much comes through subconsciously.

I also did all of Arnold's handwriting. Handwritten text in general can have a lot of emotional power and charm. Like a handwritten letter, it's much more personal and individual than typeset text. There's also a sense of immediacy because you can't cut-and-paste or delete paragraphs; you only write and that's that.

The "crinkled scraps of paper" design was to make sure the graphics were set apart somehow so they didn't just look like illustrations drawn straight from the text. The look makes clear that Arnold doesn't have a nice, shiny sketchbook, but instead collects his artwork on scraps of paper.

What did you take away from this project?
I got to stretch my repertoire and deal with material that I wouldn't have come up with on my own. I really wanted to do justice to the story, Junior, Sherman, and to the complex issues Sherman evoked so beautifully with his words. The manuscript is so rich and vivid; I couldn't help but think, "What a task!" Doing this work was like running a marathon, eating a big rich feast, and walking into creepy basements with a candle.

My dad got a copy of the book as soon as it came out. He'd read a review that said he'd laugh and cry, which he of course shrugged off as marketing pap. The next day, he called me to say that he'd chuckled out loud and teared up a few times by the end. He was amazed.

Diary has struck a chord with so many people, in so many different ways. It's accessible to all ages, all sorts of people. It's an honor to be a part of a work that so many people find inspirational.

Discussion Guide

1. Consider the adjectives "absolutely true" and "part-time." What concepts appear to be emphasized by the images and the title? Does the cover make a reference to Junior's internal struggle, or a struggle between Junior and the white power structure, or both, or neither?

2. By drawing cartoons, Junior feels safe. He draws "because I want to talk to the world. And I want the world to pay attention to me." How do Junior's cartoons (for example, "Who my parents would have been if somebody had paid attention to their dreams" and "white, white, white, white, white, white, white, white" and "white/Indian") show his understanding of the ways that racism has deeply impacted his and his family's lives?

3. When Junior is in Reardan (the little white town), he is "half Indian," and when he is in Wellpinit (his home reservation), he is "half white."

"It was like being Indian was my job," he says, "but it was only a part-time job. And it didn't pay well at all." At Reardan High, why does Junior pretend to have more money than he does, even though he knows that "lies have short shelf lives"?

4. Junior describes his home reservation as "located approximately one million miles north of Important and two billion miles west of Happy." Yet when he and Rowdy look down from almost the top of an immense pine, he says, "We could see our entire world. And our entire world, at that moment, was green and golden and perfect." What forces drive the dichotomy of Junior's perceptions of his world and allow him to see the land in apparently disparate ways?

5. Cultural outsiders who write young adult fiction tend to romanticize the impoverishment of Indians. Junior is having none of this: "It sucks to be poor, and it sucks to feel that you somehow *deserve* to be poor. You start believing that you're poor because you're stupid and ugly. And then you start believing that you're stupid and ugly because you're Indian. And because you're Indian you start believing that you're destined to be poor. It's an ugly circle and *there's nothing you can do about it*. Poverty doesn't give you strength or teach you lessons about perseverance. No, poverty only teaches you how to be poor." How does Junior's direct language address this stereotypical portrayal of Indians? What about his language draws the teen reader into the realities of his life?

6. Junior's parents, Rowdy's father, and others in their community are addicted to alcohol, and Junior's white "friend with potential," Penelope, has bulimia. "There are all kinds of addicts, I guess," he says. "We all have pain. And we all look for ways to make the pain go away." Compared to the characters in Jon Hassler's young adult novel, *Jemmy* (Atheneum, 1980), how does Junior's understanding of addiction transcend ethnicity and class?

7. Junior refers to his home reservation as "the rez," a familiar name for the place in which he was born, the place in which his friends and relatives for many generations back were born and are buried, and the land to which he is tied that, no matter how bad things get, will now and forever be called "home." What would Junior think of a cultural outsider, such as Ian Frazier, who visits a reservation to gather material for a book and then calls his book *On the Rez*?

8. At Junior's grandmother's funeral, held on the football field to accommodate all the people who loved her, Junior's mother publicly gives a white billionaire his comeuppance to the delight of the whole community. "And then my mother started laughing," Junior says. "And that set us all off. It was the most glorious noise I'd ever heard. And I realized that, sure, Indians were drunk and sad and displaced and crazy and mean but, dang, we knew how to laugh. When it comes to death, we know that laughter and tears are pretty much the same thing. And so, laughing and crying, we said goodbye to my grandmother. And when we said goodbye to one grandmother, we said goodbye to all of them. Each funeral was a funeral for all of us. We lived and died together." How does this story reflect a cultural insider's perspective and how does it disrupt stereotypes about stoic Indians?

9. "I'm fourteen years old and I've been to forty-two funerals," Junior says. "That's really the biggest difference between Indians and white people." In the community of Wellpinit, everyone is related, everyone is valued, everyone lives a hardscrabble life, everyone is at risk for early death, and the loss of one person is a loss to the community. Compare Wellpinit to Reardan, whose residents have greater access to social services, health care, and wealth, and people are socially distanced from each other. How does Junior use this blunt, matter-of-fact statement to describe this vast gulf between an impoverished Indian community and a middle-class white town just a few miles away?

10. In many ways, Junior is engulfed by the emotional realities of his life and his community. Yet his spare, matter-of-fact language and his keen sense of irony help him to confront and negotiate the hurt, the rage, and the senselessness of Wellpinit's everyday realities. How does Junior use language to lead readers, whose lives may be very different from his own, to the kind of understanding that they will not necessarily get from other young adult fiction, whose writers do not have this same kind of lived experience?

11. Cultural markers can be defined as the behaviors, speech patterns, ways of seeing the world, ethics, and principles that identify a person as belonging to a particular culture. When Rowdy and Junior play one-on-one at the end of the book—and they don't keep score—how is their friendship solidified by their deep knowing of who they are and what they come from?

As they expected more of me, I expected more of myself, and it just grew and grew.